THE HORSE CONNECTION PART 1

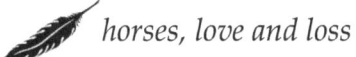 *horses, love and loss*

I0547608

THE HORSE CONNECTION PART 1: *horses, love and loss*

© 2025 Charlotte Godfrey
All rights reserved
ISBN 979-8-9913993-3-3
ENOLA PUBLISHING LLC
A previous version of this book was published in 2014 under the title
DRESSAGE LESSONS © 2014 Charlotte Godfrey
It has been revised, re-written, and re-named to become the first novel of
THE HORSE CONNECTION series

BARN HELP
   the making of a murderer
Was the 2nd publication in the Centerline Farm series
All rights reserved
ENOLA PUBLISHING LLC

THE HORSE CONNECTION is a work of fiction. The characters in this book are fictional, and not based on any person, living or dead, with the exception of Craig Heckert, owner of Rivervale Farm. Any other resemblance to any person living or dead is entirely coincidental. Some of the locations and events in this book are real and the Nokota horse is a real breed.

To learn more about Craig Heckert and Rivervale Farm go to:
http://www.rivervalefarm.com
To learn more about the Nokota horse go to:
http://en.wikipedia.org/wiki/Nokota_horse

TABLE OF CONTENTS

BARN HELP
Layne's early years

FALLING IN LOVE
Marsha's story

ABOUT DRESSAGE

Dressage is a French term. Basically, it means training. The goal of dressage is to make the horse a willing partner in obedience and precision of movement. Dressage, done properly, also contributes to the mental and physical health of horses and their riders.

The training of a dressage horse progresses through levels. The purpose of the levels of training is to guide and test the progression of training, which can potentially go all the way to Olympic level.

Dressage shows are a method of testing and judging the training of horse and rider as they progress up the levels.

The USDF (United States Dressage Federation) provides tests for Introductory through Fourth Level. Each level consists of 3 tests. Above Forth Level, dressage competitions use tests written by the FEI (Federation Equestre Internationale.) FEI dressage tests are used world-wide and in the Olympics. All dressage tests are scored by the percentage of points achieved in each test.

Riders are able to earn awards and medals as they progress up the levels. Horses can earn awards and certificates.

In the past, dressage was an English style sport, but Western dressage has become popular and is now a USEF (United States Equestrian Federation) sanctioned sport. Dressage became an Olympic sport in 1912.

To learn more about American dressage, in the English style, go to http://www.usdf.org.
To learn more about Western Dressage, go to http://www. usef.org. Search for "Western Dressage."

SOME DEFINITIONS

BREECHES: Riding pants. The riding pants favored by most dressage riders are "full seat" breeches. They are reinforced along the seat and down the inner legs to the calf or ankle. Full seat breeches provide grip and protection when riders sit the gaits of dressage horses.

CHESTNUT, SORREL, BAY, GRAY, GRULLO, ETC: are words referring to the colors of horses. See http://en.wikipedia.org/wiki/Equine_coat_color for more information.

CLINIC: A day or days of lessons for riders and spectators. Clinics are usually given by well-known instructors or experts in the equine industry. Some clinics are commercial in nature, designed to sell a product.

FEATHERS: Long hair found on the back of the legs of some horses and ponies.

GELDING: A castrated male horse.

MARE: A female horse over the age of 5 years. A female horse under the age of 5 years is called a filly.

PADDOCK: A small enclosure for a horse or horses, with or without grass. A pasture is a larger enclosure for horses with grass for grazing.

SHEATH: The pocket of skin surrounding the penis of a male horse or gelding.

TEMPI CHANGES: In the canter, horses push off with a hind leg and land on a diagonal fore leg. Switching the diagonals is called a flying change. Tempi changes are multiple flying changes in a row such as changing every stride, every second stride, every third stride, or every fourth stride.

BARN HELP

DEDICATION

*For Judy Dowling who taught me how to care
for horses, and for the feelings of others.*

1 - IN TROUBLE AGAIN

I worked at Ironwood Ranch for two years, and I got fired four times. Each time, it was over something stupid.

The first time I got fired, it was over a barn door.

I was only 12 years old at the time, too young to legally work, so the barn owner paid me under the table. It was poor pay for all the work I did, but I had to work, and I didn't want to work anywhere except around horses.

Our whole family worked, except for my dad. My mother baby-sat and cleaned other people's houses and my two brothers, Tommy and Danny, cut lawns in the summer, shoveled snow in the winter, painted and cleaned out junk for people, and did anything they could during the winter. My baby brother was too young to do anything but be a baby.

Anyway, I got fired for leaving the barn door open when it was time to bring the horses in. It was my first day at Ironwood Ranch, and nobody told me to shut the barn door. The other kid I worked with should have told me that it was my responsibility because I had cleaned the stalls by the barn door that day. But he didn't. I think he didn't on purpose.

Anyway, so when it was time to run the horses in

from the field, guess what? Half of them went into their stalls and half of them ran out the door, down the driveway, down the road and, well, you get the picture.

It took two hours to round them all up, and I got fired. For three days. I guess they missed me. I've always been a hard worker, and I'm a good rider. I'll ride any horse. I get along with most of them and always settle the difficult ones, so I guess they needed me.

The second time I got fired, it was because I got my period and I thought I was dying, so I didn't go to work. When my mom found me in the outhouse crying because I was bleeding to death, she slapped me, told me to stop crying, and gave me a tampon.

"Congratulations," she said. "Now you can get pregnant and become a slave to a man and your children!"

"What? I don't want to do that!"

"Then stay away from men," she told me. "Don't let them get between your legs."

"So, I'm not dying?"

"No, you've just got the curse. It will happen once a month until you're in your forties or fifties. Congratulations. Welcome to womanhood. Stick this up yourself and go back to work. You'll need more, and you can buy them at the drugstore. They're called tampons."

Then my mother smiled. She didn't smile much.

"You're pretty," she said. "You're gonna have a lot of trouble with men unless you're tough."

"Great. Well, I can handle men."

"Now that you can get pregnant, if you don't bleed once a month, you'd better worry. That's why women called their period their friend."

"I thought you said it was a curse."

"That's right. It's a curse, and it's your friend. It's your friend because it means you're not pregnant. It's a curse because it's nasty, and you get it every month."

"Well, that sounds awful."

"Being a woman is no party. It's hard."

"Every woman gets it?"

"Yep. Until you're forty or fifty. You say, 'I got my friend,' and other women know what you mean."

"Wonderful," I said, sighing.

"Now, get off your pity pony and get back to work."

When I went back to Ironwood Ranch the next day, they sent me back home for missing work. I guess they knew I would hate that. Then they called Mom and told her to send me back to work on Monday. I screaamed and went back to the woodpile to chop wood until Monday.

I've always had a bad temper. My older brother, Tommy, said I would bite him when I was younger. Mom said I was just born angry. She said I wouldn't cry, even as a baby. I would just scream with rage.

I can't remember much about being a baby, but I

know I have a bad temper. It takes a little while for me to lose it, but when the pot boils over, and I lose my cool, I am truly angry. Always been like that. All my life. I throw things and hit stuff, sometimes people.

But not animals. I love animals. They don't try to get a person upset. Only people do that.

So I finally lost it with that stupid, lazy fart I worked with at Ironwood Ranch. And I got fired. Again.

I probably wouldn't have gotten fired the third time if I hadn't thrown a muck bucket of manure at that asshole Jimmie. And if he wasn't the boss's son. But I did, and he was.

So I went home, and then I had to sit around and listen to my dad tell me what a failure I was and how I'd never amount to anything. But he knew the boss would forgive me and call me back to work. I'm the best worker he's had on the farm. He said that. So I would get hired back. I just had to wait until he called my parents to send me back on Monday, like always.

And he did, so I went back to work. But when I broke Jimmie's arm for touching me, I got fired for the fourth time, and they didn't call me back.

I didn't tell my parents what happened. I just told them I got fired and they said okay and waited for the boss to call me back. But I knew they wouldn't call me back that time.

I was worried that I would have to babysit or clean houses, I couldn't do that. I couldn't work cutting lawns, either. So, I was miserable.

By the end of the week, my mother figured out what happened even though I still hadn't told her. She was at the grocery store and Jimmie and his mother were there. My mother got behind them in the checkout line.

"Hi Mrs. Williams," she said, "and Jimmie." She acknowledged Jimmie, too. My mother was just trying to be nice.

Mrs. Williams looked at my mother and sniffed.

"Oh, what happened to your arm, Jimmie?" Jimmie's arm was in a cast. Mom was truly surprised. Like I said, she didn't know.

Jimmie dropped his head, and his mother said, "You know damn well what happened to Jimmie's arm! Your little bitch daughter broke it! I should sue you!"

"Really? I didn't know. My daughter doesn't cry to her mama when things happen. Maybe little Jimmie darlin' put his hand in the wrong place?"

Mrs. Williams grabbed Jimmie's good arm and rushed out of the grocery store, pulling Jimmie behind her.

When my mother got home, she found me at the woodshed, chopping wood. There was a lot of wood chopped already for winter. More than enough for us, but my father could sell the excess. It was the only thing he did to make money, so I was just trying to help out until I found another job.

"Well done," my mother said.

"I didn't chop all of it," I told her.

"I mean you taught Jimmie Williams a good lesson!"

"He put his hand on me, so I broke it. I got fired."

My mother laughed and said, "You won't be working there anymore!"

"Dad will be mad."

"Dad won't be told what happened unless Jimmie's parents tell him. Then I would pity them! Your dad will go off on them."

"What about the money? I know I need to work."

"I heard the Silver Spur is looking for help. Go there tomorrow."

I was only thirteen by then, but I had worked in barns since I was eight years old, first with cows and with horses after that. I rode horses, mucked stalls and took care of almost everything in the barns I worked at.

I was strong and tough, and I guess that was a good thing since my dad couldn't keep a job. He was a Vietnam veteran, and he drank too much. So Mom, me and my brothers had to work. Mom worked six days a week, and my brothers and I worked after school.

But I always got into trouble at work. Usually with the other workers. I was always mad about something or at someone.

My first job was working in a cow barn when I was eight years old. I hated it. Cows are stupid. And messy. They had a few horses there, and I took care of them too. I liked that. Horses smell good and their poop is cleaner. And I liked to ride them when my work with the cows was done.

When I was ten, I got the chance to work with just horses at a farm called Chaps. I was a good rider by then, and I helped break out a lot of horses at Chap's before I even knew I was doing a professional's work. To me, it was just fun.

My mother said I was a natural-born worker. I didn't understand why the other workers were so lazy. They left most of the work for me to do, and they just played around. I didn't like that, and after I had been there a few weeks, I went to the boss and complained.

I found him in the round pen, working with a colt.

"I won't pick up the slack for those two girls anymore," I yelled at him.

Mr. Bob, that's what we called him, put his lunge whip down and walked over to the round pen rails.

"What's going on, Layne?"

"I won't clean the stalls they don't clean, and I won't be the one left to water and sweep when they leave for the day. Not unless I'm paid more than them," I said, a little quieter.

"I didn't know that was going on," he said. "I thought you were just slower than them. You've been doing their work?"

"Yeah. They just play around a lot, throw things at each other and laugh. They don't clean their share of the stalls or do any feeding, and I'm tired of it."

The boss decided to let the other girls go and keep me. I had to do all the work then, but I got paid more. My dad liked that, but it cut into the time I had left to ride.

After a few months of that, I went back to the boss. "I don't want to clean that many stalls anymore," I said. "I want to ride."

Mr. Bob just looked at me and shook his head. "What makes you think you can ride?"

I sat on his young horses or horses he was training while he lunged them, but I guess he didn't know I rode his horses by myself whenever I got the chance.

"I'm a damn good rider," I said.

"You're good enough to help me, I'll admit that, but your job is to clean stalls and feed and water. The riding at this barn is training. You aren't a trainer."

"I can ride, and I can train," I insisted.

"Can you ride Redman?" Mr. Bob smiled, thinking he had me.

Redman was a horse that had come to Chaps for training. He was five years old and strong. He liked to push me around when I handled him, taking him out to the turnout pen and bringing him back in. He was also restless in his stall and usually tore up the bedding in it.

I finally had him figured out, though. He was a smart horse, and he was just bored. When Mr. Bob had him for a month, and still hadn't ridden him, I asked him, "When will you start riding Redman?"

"I'll ride him when he settles down a bit," he said. "He's too wired up, tearing up his stall and giving anybody who handles him a hard time."

That's when I started playing games with Redman. I taught him hand signals. I taught him to pay attention to what my hands told him and, when he did what they told him, he got a small handful of grain that I kept in my pocket.

Redman loved playing games. I taught him to move left, move right, back up, move forward and bow so I could get on his back. Then I transferred the hand signals to my feet and legs. When he understood all that, I rode him in circles in his stall.

I couldn't tell Mr. Bob I did that, though. Redman was at the barn for Mr. Bob to saddle-break. But when he dared me to ride him, I said, "Sure, I'll ride Redman."

Mr. Bob's smile melted off his face. "Shee-it," he said. "You can't ride Redman."

"Yes, I can."

"No. He's too hot. You can't ride him. You'll get yourself hurt."

"He's not hot. He's just smart."

Mr. Bob frowned at me. "Look, you're just a kid. You think you know it all, but I've been in this horse business all my life. You can't ride Redman."

"I already rode him."

Mr. Bob's face got tight, and then he got nasty. "You shouldn't be tellin' lies, Layne."

"I rode him."

"Yeah, right. Get your stuff and get out of here." Mr. Bob reached into his jeans pocket and pulled out some bills. "Here's your pay. Get out of here."

So I got fired from Chaps.

It took me a while to understand why I was let go, and it took me longer to stop being angry about it.

After that, I got the job at Ironwood Ranch, and you know what happened there.

When I got the job at The Silver Spur, I knew I had to tone it down a little, and do some of the menial labor, as well as ride the horses. I decided to try and keep my temper in check and get along with the other workers.

But life had other plans for me, I guess, because I got into trouble again.

2 - TROUBLE AT THE SILVER SPUR

I pretended to be asleep in the backseat. We had been in the crew cab truck for almost an hour. It was probably 6 pm or later. I didn't know. I was in the back seat of the truck, and had laid down for a quick nap before we picked up hay. I didn't know that Ray was up to no good. I just wanted to take a nap. But it turned out that trying to take a nap was the right thing to do because that rotten bastard Ray was up to no good big time.

I had watched him with my peripheral vision when he put his hand over the top of my drink can. I knew that wasn't good. I thought he probably dropped a bug or poop in it, until I heard him say, "It worked," to Joe, who was sitting beside him in the front seat of the truck.

After I watched Ray put something in my drink with my peripheral vision (you get real good at watching out of the corners of your eyes when you work with horses, especially young horses who like to sneak up on you and deliver a quick bite or kick, just for fun), I pretended to drink the rest of it, plugging the pop top hole with my tongue and then I made a show of tossing it into the garbage bin at the end of the barn aisle.

After watching me toss the pop can, Ray said, "Come on Layne, Max wants us to go get a load of hay." Then he and Joe walked to the barn door and waited for me.

My boss, Max, sent us to get hay once a week, so that was nothing unusual. I put the pitchfork down and parked the wheelbarrow I had been using in an empty stall. Then I met them outside by the old crew cab truck we used to haul hay.

I didn't suspect anything really, so I put my head down on the seat to grab a few minutes of sleep. I always fell asleep in the back seat of moving vehicles because, between school and work and helping Mom at home, then doing enough homework to get passing grades at school, I got very little sleep. But when he drove past the road to the hay farm, I started putting things together in my mind and I thought: what the heck?

I pretended to be asleep long after he had gone past the road to the hay farm. I didn't know what Ray was doing but I knew it was no good, and I had figured out by then that he had put something in my drink to make me sleep. When he leaned toward Joe and said, "It worked. She's sound asleep," I thought, "You jerk! I'll get you."

I watched them through a little opening in my eyes. Joe looked back at me from the passenger seat, but said nothing.

"Yeah," Ray said. "This is gonna be fun. We can teach her a lesson and get our rocks off too. The cabin's not far from here I'm gonna stop and get us some beer."

I stopped breathing when I heard that. Bastards! I knew they were scum, and I had always treated them like it. So they were gonna teach me a lesson? Maybe I could teach them something.

Finally, when it seemed like we had been on the road for hours, Ray slowed the truck down and pulled off the road. I could see by slightly peeking with my right eye that he had stopped at a convenience store.

Ray gave Joe a knife. "Watch her," he said.

"Aw, man, I gotta pee," Joe whined.

"Hold it!" Ray jumped out of the truck and Joe stayed put until Ray went into the store. After I heard the bell on the store's door jingle, Ray looked over the seat at me. I had parted my lips and was breathing slowly, pretending I was asleep. "Shee-it," he moaned, and a second later he left the truck.

He was either headed to the john or gonna pee by the truck's tire. I knew he was a little slow, mentally, and it would take him a minute to decide what to do with the knife in his hand before he could unzip, so I opened the crew cab door just enough to slide out of the truck.

I left the door open. I figured I had five minutes or less while he peed. Maybe sooner than that before Ray returned.

I bolted toward the back of the store. There was nothing but an open field behind the store.

I slid behind the dumpster parked behind the store

and heard Ray and Joe yelling at each other. Then they started looking for me. The dummies were shouting at each other, so I knew where they were. One of them went into the store and the other checked the rest room on the side of the building, so I bolted back to the truck and waited a minute.

The idiots came out of the store and the rest room at the same time. Ray was still clinging to the beer. "She's gotta be out there!" He pointed to the field behind the store. "You go that way," he told Joe, and he ran around the other side of the store.

I jumped into the truck. The keys weren't in the ignition, so I reached under the steering wheel and grabbed the wires that always hung down there and touched them together like I'd seen it done whenever Ray lost or forgot the keys or was just too lazy to go get them, which was almost all the time. The truck started, I slammed it into reverse, backed out of the parking lot, and shifted it into drive and got out of there. I left those two assholes behind. Let them explain it to Max.

I stopped at the hay barn on the way back, loaded 30 bales of hay and drove back to the Silver Spur. I parked the truck in front of the barn, got on my bike and left.

I went to work the next day after school, as usual, grabbed my wheelbarrow and pitchfork and started on the first stall. I was working on the second one when the idiots appeared in the doorway of the stall. I was trapped.

"Hey, thanks for getting the hay for us yesterday," Ray said. "And it was really nice of you to give us the rest of the afternoon off."

I just looked at him while the anger was building up inside me.

"Yeah, Max was a little upset with you, though," Ray said with a smirk on his face. "He thought you were getting a little uppity, taking over like that, and acting like you was the boss. And you owe us," he added, "or else we will tell Max you dumped us just to be a bitch when we left the truck to go pee."

Then Ray turned to Joe. "Wanna go first?"

Joe smiled and shook his head. "Go ahead, bro. You go first."

Ray stepped into the stall. Then he spread his legs and unbuckled his belt.

I didn't ask him what he was doing. I just hit him hard on his stupid head with the business end of my pitchfork. I was really glad it was the old-fashioned metal kind. But Ray wasn't. He crumbled like an empty burlap sack.

Joe was a little slow to react. He just stood there with his mouth open, watching Ray fall. That gave me enough time to grab the wheelbarrow and slam it into his knees. He fell as gracelessly as his bro. Just for fun, I emptied the contents of the wheelbarrow on his face.

I didn't stick around after that. I grabbed my bicycle and went home. It was Friday, so I told my mother we ran out of work early and quit for the day.

I didn't work at the Silver Spur on the weekends. The boys were going to get a couple of days to think about things. I just hoped they were smart enough to figure out that I won't be messed with when I went back to work on Monday.

But Max called my mother and said I was fired.

By then, I guess she had enough of me getting fired, because that's when she decided to get rid of me.

3 - AUNT MAE

Mom found me at the woodpile again.

"I'm sending you to live with my sister in Nisland," she said. "There's a nice horse farm not too far from where she lives. You can get a job there."

"What sister in Nisland? You have a sister?" Mom never told me she had a sister.

"You never met her. Her name's Mae," was all she said.

I was stunned. I had an aunt. I had an aunt that I had to go live with. Her name was Mae.

"Mom! I don't want to leave! I'm sorry I lost my job! Please don't make me go. I'll get another job. I promise! I can wash cars or something." I grabbed my mother and hugged her.

"Nonsense!" My mother pushed me away. You have to leave someday. And horses are the only thing you love. You won't get another job with horses here. I hope you can get a job at the farm there."

"Mom, I love you."

Mom shifted my baby brother from her left hip to her right. "More than horses?" My baby brother started to cry, so Mom bounced him a little.

I hesitated before answering. Mom would want the truth. "Maybe just as much."

"You're going. Go pack your stuff."

I opened my mouth to protest, but my mother stopped me. "Not another word. Go!" She turned and walked back into the house.

My stuff wasn't much. A few pairs of jeans. T-shits, tennis shoes, socks, and three pairs of barn boots. A winter coat, coveralls and two worn jackets. I had a couple of paperbacks and, I shoved them into my duffle bag. Underwear. Deodorant. That was new. And those awful tampons. We tied my bike to the back of the car. That was it.

I didn't know that my mom was planning to leave my dad when she took me to my aunt's house in Rivervale. It took most of the day to get there, and she never said a word about it. I can't remember us saying anything. I just looked out the window or tried to amuse my baby brother when he started fussing.

Aunt Mae's house was on the edge of town. It was small, white and had a grey roof that was missing a few shingles. The grass needed cutting and the steps to the porch were worn. My mother knocked on the door and waited. She knocked again.

"I'm comin', dammit," someone yelled from the back of the house. Then we felt footsteps vibrate the porch floor as the person who cussed at us came closer.

The door burst open, and my Aunt Mae stood there, dirty blouse hanging outside her jeans, her hand on her hip. "Well, I'll be damned! It's Laura and her brats! What do you want?"

My mother said, "Well, hello to you too, Mae. Glad to see you. Can we come in?"

Mae opened the door and bowed to my mom. "My home is your home," she said. "Just what I wanted. Company."

"Thanks, Mae," Mom said, and my little brother started crying. Mom bounced him on her hip.

"Is that the last one you're having?" Mae pointed to my baby brother.

"This is Buddy," Mom said. "Buddy, meet Mae." Mom turned Buddy around to look at Aunt Mae and he held his head up long enough to stare at her for a minute, then broke out crying again.

Mom laid Buddy on her shoulder and bounced him. "I brought Layne to you," Mom said. "She's a hard worker and there's a horse farm not far from here. She can work there and pay you rent."

"Yeah?" Aunt Mae said. "What makes you think I want a roommate?"

"You're our only family, and we need your help," Mom said.

"Huh! Like I'm in any position to help anyone. Why do you need my help?"

"I'm leaving Jim," my mother said.

I opened my mouth and turned to look at my mother.

"Don't say anything," my mother warned me.

"I have two bigger boys and Buddy to worry about. Layne is self-sufficient. She can work and help you around the house. Painting and weeding. Like that. She can fix your porch and put some shingles on your roof. She's not much good for housework or cooking, but it looks like you aren't either."

I was shocked when my Aunt Mae laughed. "Never was," she said. "Where are you going with your boys?"

"A shelter, I guess. What else can I do?"

"You can git them and your sorry ars up here, that's what," my Aunt Mae said and marched into the kitchen to make a pot of coffee. So that was that.

Mom would have to go back and get her stuff and the boys, but at least we had a place to stay, and she could probably work in town.

"Thank you, Mae," Mom said. "I'll go back and pack what I can and be back with the boys by the weekend. I know I can get everyone and our stuff out of the house when he has his doctor's appointment on Saturday. I'll be back Saturday night."

"Okay," Aunt Mae said. And that was that.

4 - NISLAND

After my mom left, Aunt Mae and I spent the afternoon cleaning out the little room at the back of the house. Mom and the boys would sleep there. Mae would keep her small bedroom by the bathroom, and I would sleep in the living room on the couch. It didn't matter to me. The only thing that mattered to me was getting a job at the horse farm.

I had turned fourteen in the Fall of that year. I was finally the legal age for an agricultural worker. That's what they call children who work on farms here in the states. In other countries, children who work are called sweat shop workers or child laborers. But now I was of legal age for an agricultural worker in the states, and that was a big relief.

All I knew was that I had to work, and I only wanted to work with horses. Not that anyone cared. But it was nice to be legal, just the same. The only thing that really mattered to me was getting to the horse farm and getting that job. With my background, I thought it would be easy.

But that didn't happen.

The school year had already begun. I was in the 9th grade, and I would have to catch the school bus every day or ride my bike to school. A bike was fine for now but, when winter came, it wouldn't be fine. Then I hoped Aunt Mae or my mother would drive me and the boys to school. Otherwise, we would have to ride the bus. But we could figure that out later.

As I said, my main concern was getting a job at Rivervale Farm, so I looked at a map and tried to figure out how long it would take me to get there if I rode my bike to school and went to the afterward. I figured I could cut southeast through town and get there within a half hour.

On Monday, I rode my bike to school, as planned, and afterward, to Rivervale Farm. I pedaled up the long driveway and left my bike at the side of the main barn.

I walked up to a girl sweeping the barn aisle. "I'm looking for Craig Heckert," I told her.

She nodded at the center of the barn. "He's riding Truman in the indoor."

I turned left and walked to the gate at the indoor arena. A slim man trotted by on a black horse. In the corner, he picked up a canter and aimed the horse toward the jump in the center of the arena. When Truman took the jump, Craig effortlessly rose from the saddle and sailed over the jump with the horse. When they landed on the other side, he sat down smoothly and turned the corner of the arena.

That's when he saw me.

"Hi," he said, nodding at me.

"Hi."

"Would you please open the gate at the end of the arena?" he asked. "I'm taking this boy outside today."

"Sure, no problem," I said and hurried to open the gate. This is a good start, I thought.

I followed Craig and Truman outside and watched them until he dismounted and brought the horse back inside. He removed the saddle and handed the reins to the girl who had been sweeping the aisle.

"Truman needs a quick brush, and he can go back outside afterward," he told her.

Then he turned to me. "I'm Craig. And you are?"

"I'm Layne. I just moved her and I'm looking for a job."

"Oh," he said. "Well, I have a lot of good help, and we aren't hiring anyone right now."

"I have 6 years' experience working with horses," I told him. "I can clean stalls, walk horses, do feeding chores and help train them," I said.

"That's impressive," Craig said, smiling. "But we don't need anyone right now. You're welcome to stay and watch for a while, though."

"Okay." I had a lump in my throat. I thought it would be easy. Just walk in and get a job.

I shoved my hands into my jeans and watched Craig put his saddle away. Then he took out a rope halter and showed it to me. "I'm going to work with one of the yearlings," he said. "Do you know how to use a rope halter?"

I held out my hand, and he gave me the halter. I draped it over my left hand and picked up the loose end with my right hand. I looped the loose end down through the halter, then brought it back toward the imaginary horse's tail, then toward to the imaginary horse's eye and back through the loop I had just created. I handed it back to Craig.

"Perfect," he said. "Let's go get a yearling."

I followed him to the back pasture and 6 young horses ran up to the fence to greet us. None of them had halters on.

"Why don't I turn my horses out with halters?" he asked me.

"Because they could get caught on something like a fence or scratch their face with a hoof and get their hoof caught in the halter. Or they could step on the halter when they are grazing and break the little bone in their nose. Once, I saw a horse break his occipital bone because his fly mask got caught on a fence post and he tried to jerk it off." I realized I was talking too much and shut up.

"Exactly," Craig said and took the halter from me.

I watched as he crawled through the fence and scratched a chestnut gelding on his withers. The young horse closed his eyes and leaned into Craig's hand. After a couple more scratches, Craig slipped the rope halter over his head and walked him down to the gate. The other 5 yearlings followed them.

I walked on the other side of the fence and met them at the gate. I released the latch and pushed the gate inward so I could use it as a barrier to keep the other yearlings from following Craig. He came through the gate with the chestnut and watched as I pulled the gate shut and latched it.

"This is Rambo," he said and turned toward the barn.

I followed them into the barn and down the aisle, where Craig tied Rambo to a ring on the wall. He used a slip knot that could be released easily by pulling the end hanging from the tie ring if the horse panicked and backed up or reared.

Craig patted the yearling's neck and walked away. I was puzzled but figured he was testing me, so I slowly bent over and picked up the rubber curry that someone left on the floor next to the gelding's legs. I finished rubbing the gelding in positive circles all over his body and looked around for more grooming tools. There was an open door on the opposite side of the aisle. I talked to the yearling as I walked behind him and went to the door. I flicked on the light switch. I had guessed right. It was a tack room. There was a grooming box on the floor and, still talking to Rambo, I found a bristle brush and flicked off the light.

Craig walked up as I was finishing the yearling's legs. He went to the tack room and grabbed a hoof pick and handed it to me without speaking.

I took the hoof pick and handed him the brush. Then I went to the yearling's right hip. I ran my right hand along his hip until I got to the hock. Then I ran my hand around his hock and down the front of his cannon bone until I reached the fetlock. I put a little pressure on the fetlock and felt Rambo resist, so I released the pressure and Rambo put more weight on his left hind leg and lifted his right hind leg for me. I moved my right hand to his pastern and turned the hoof up, picked a little dirt out of his hoof, and released it.

Rambo put his hoof down and turned his head slightly and watched me as I put my hand on his hip and walked behind him to his left side. Once again, only this time with my left hand, I ran my hand down his hip, around his hock, down the front of his cannon bone and to his fetlock. When he shifted his weight to his right hind leg, I slid my hand down to his pastern and lifted his hoof, picked out the dirt in his frog and released it.

"Good boy," I said quietly.

Then I went to his shoulder and ran my left hand down his leg, past the knee and down to his cannon bone. Once again, the yearling shifted his weight for me, and I was able to lift his pastern and clean his hoof. I stood, stroked his neck, and walked around him and stood on his right side. Rambo knew what I wanted, shifted his weight and lifted his right front hoof before I could ask him. "Good boy," I crooned softly. I picked the frog clean, lowered the hoof and stroked his neck.

Craig said nothing, but he took the hoof pick from me and handed me a comb. I understood that he wanted me to comb out Rambo's mane and tail.

I took the comb and looked around for a grooming product. There was a bottle of silicone lubricant spray sitting against the wall. I picked it up and, turning away from Rambo, sprayed both hands and the comb with it. Then I rubbed my hands through his short tail, sprayed them again, and rubbed my hands through his mane. I picked up the comb again and, starting at the ends of his mane, combed through it until I could comb roots to ends without encountering a snarl.

I did the same with his tail. I combed end to top, working out any snarl the comb encountered with my fingers. It took a few minutes to finish Rambo's tail, and Craig watched in silence, leaning against the wall.

When I was finished, I turned to Craig. He said nothing. He just released the tie and led Rambo into the arena where he walked the yearling in a circle to the left around himself.

Occasionally, and only when Rambo was watching him, Craig tossed the end of the lead rope between the yearling's legs or swung it in a circle. Rambo watched and kept walking. When Craig tossed the end of the lead rope on Rambo's back, the yearling moved away a step, but didn't panic. The second time Craig tossed the rope on his back, Rambo ignored it.

Craig turned to me and said, "Here. You do the other side."

Most horses have to be taught things on both sides of their body. Maybe it is because their eyes are on the sides of their head. Maybe it's just the way they learn. I knew of only one horse that could transfer knowledge from one side of her body to the other without having to be taught on both sides. So I understood what Craig was telling me.

I took the lead rope and walked to the other side of the gelding's body. His eyes followed me and did not look at Craig. That was good. I knew he understood that I would be directing him now.

I asked Rambo to walk forward, but he did not understand the word "walk" so I turned my body slightly in the direction I wanted him to go and tugged a little on the lead rope. He moved forward and slightly in toward me for a couple of steps. "Good," I crooned. Then I walked forward again while tugging slightly on the lead rope and saying the word "w-a-l-k" in a drawn-out manner.

Rambo's ears moved forward as if to say, "What?" I repeated my walk, the tug and the word "w-a-l-k." Rambo walked forward.

"Good," I said. I asked him to walk again, and he understood and walked forward. When I stopped walking, he stopped. I asked him to "w-a-l-k" again, and he did.

Soon, the yearling was walking around me as I stood in the middle of the circle with only my body pointing slightly in the direction he should go.

Then I said, "Ho." Rambo's ears focused on me, but he did not stop walking. I gave a slight tug on the lead rope and repeated, "Ho." Rambo stopped walking and looked at me.

"Good boy," I said. I asked him to walk again and "Ho" again. He got another "Good boy."

Then I walked in front of Rambo and stood on his left side. His ears and head followed me, but he didn't move. Craig had moved to the arena wall sometime while I was working on Rambo's right side, and he leaned there and watched us.

I pointed my body slightly left and said "w-a-l-k" and made a little tug on the lead rope. Rambo walked forward and in a circle around me to the left. When I said "Ho," he turned his ears and his head to me. I had stopped walking, and he stopped walking. I asked him to walk on again, using the lead rope and my body position as a clue, and he did as I asked, and stopped walking when I said, "Ho."

Then I tugged slightly on the lead rope and Rambo started walking, but I kept the tension on the lead rope and soon the yearling was passing me and walking in a circle to the right. I said, "Good boy." When I said, "Ho," he stopped walking.

Then I walked up to him, stroked his neck, and said, "You're a good boy."

I led Rambo over to Craig and handed him the lead rope. Craig pushed off the wall and led the yearling out of the arena without saying a word to me.

5 - RIVERVALE FARM

I went back to the farm the next day and left my bike on the side of the barn. Craig was nowhere in sight, so I helped the young girl I met the day before sweep the barn aisles and fill water buckets. Then we went outside and filled water troughs in the pastures. Most of the horses lived outside until winter. Only horses in training and those being shown came inside every night, she told me.

Her name was Jodie. She was sixteen and had worked for Craig since she was fourteen. "I'm fourteen," I told her.

"Well good," she said. "I'll be leaving when I turn seventeen and Craig will need another worker. I'm going to New York to do some modeling, and then, after that, I'll go to California to become an actress!"

"Wow," I said. "That's great. You must have some good connections?"

"I hope so," she frowned and shut off the water hydrant. "This place is nowhere. Nothing to do. No future."

"Well, I guess it depends on what you want," I said. "Craig certainly made a name for himself in the middle of nowhere. He has his gold medal, and he breeds great warmbloods."

"Yeah. I took lessons from him since I was 5 years old. Horses are fun, but they're a ton of work, and you can't make a lot of money with horses. Sure, once in a while someone gets lucky and breeds or trains a superstar, but that doesn't last long and it's still a hard life."

"Yeah. Most trainers have spent more time and money educating themselves than doctors have," I said.

Jodie sighed and scratched her head. "True. I want something more." She flipped her long brown hair over her shoulder and shrugged. "Let's finish getting the horses in so I can go home and get a hot shower?"

"Okay. Just tell me what to do and where they go."

I didn't see Craig, but Jodie said he came into the barn while we were bringing the horses in. She said he nodded to her, saw that we were bringing the horses in and left.

"Craig always comes out to help me bring them in," Jodie said, "but he saw you were here, and he went back into the house. He's probably doing the books. It's the end of the month and all that stuff needs to be done." Jodie wrinkled her nose. "Bookkeeping and taxes, yuck!"

I smiled and thought maybe Craig just needed some time to himself, but it was good that he came out to help her bring the horses in. It's always a good idea to have 2 people handling horses. Just a safety thing. I decided to leave my bike in front of the barn tomorrow so Craig would know I was here.

Craig owned warmblood stallions and bred Appaloosa sport horses. "How many broodmares are here?" I asked Jodie.

"It varies," she said. "Sometimes six or seven, sometimes more. He breeds to outside mares too. But they usually go home to have their foals."

I had been at school since the beginning of the week. By Wednesday, I knew how long it would take me to get to school on my bike, how long it took me to get to Rivervale, and how much time I needed to get my homework done.

My mother still hadn't returned with the boys, but she said she wouldn't be back until the weekend. So I had plenty of time to settle into a routine at school and work.

But Aunt Mae was another matter. I didn't mind sleeping on the couch and I didn't mind not getting a shower every night. The only problem was, I didn't know how to live with her. She didn't cook, didn't watch TV, and didn't care for housework, as far as I could tell. She wore coveralls every day of the week and smelled like a cow. Not a bad smell, but definitely not a "girly" smell.

Aunt Mae worked at a dairy farm. She had to be there twice a day, seven days a week, to feed, milk and clean up after a herd of 300 cows. Of course, she had help, but her days were long, and she was always tired.

Once in a while, she took a day off. Otherwise, she had to run her errands and do other things (like getting me enrolled in school) during the middle of her workday.

I appreciated Aunt Mae letting us live with her. I wanted to help her as much as possible, so I washed whatever dishes were in the sink, whatever clothes were in the laundry basket, and I swept the floor. After we patched the roof and repaired the front steps, we were pretty much done with the house.

So, I didn't ask her to drive me to school or pick me up in the afternoon. I rode my bike because I would need it to get to the barn after school, anyway. Maybe my mother could dive me to school in the winter, or maybe I would have to ride the bus. I would figure all that out later.

In the meantime, I rode my bike to school, and after school, to the farm.

It wasn't until Wednesday, my third day at the farm, that Jodie asked me why I was coming to the farm every day.

"To work, why else?" I said.

"Yeah, but you're not getting paid," Jodie wrinkled her nose at me. "Craig said he doesn't need any more help, so I don't get it. I wouldn't work my butt off every afternoon if I wasn't getting paid."

I tried to hide my disappointment. I shrugged and said, "Horses are all I care about."

"Huh! Suit yourself," Jodie said.

But I was disappointed. I thought I had been hired.

I thought Craig's testing me about the rope halter, the grooming, and the groundwork meant I had been hired. Oh well, I thought. I'll show him. So I continued to ride my bike to the barn and leave it by the barn door so he would know I was there every afternoon.

Fortunately, the barn wasn't too far from the school and the school wasn't too far from Aunt Mae's house. And winter seemed really far away.

When I got to the barn on Thursday, Jodie was waiting for me. "Hey, since you like to work with horses, I saved half the stalls for you," she said.

I folded my arms and looked at her. "Thanks," I said, "but cleaning stalls, sweeping aisles and filling water buckets isn't working with horses."

Then Craig walked into the barn. He motioned to me and turned on his heel. I guessed he wanted me to follow him. I shrugged at Jodie and followed Craig to the yearling pasture.

When he got to the pasture, he stopped at the gate and turned around. "I've been watching you," he said. "You come here every afternoon."

I nodded.

"After school, I assume?"

I nodded again.

"You've been helping Jodie finish up her chores and bringing the horses in?"

Another nod.

"Well, I've got a lot of work to do around here," he said. "I've got stallions, broodmares, weanlings, yearlings, young horses, and show horses."

I gulped. I was probably in trouble again. And without the possibility of being fired. I really did have a talent for getting in trouble, I was thinking.

"I don't have a lot of barn help," Craig went on. "I prefer to work with the horses by myself."

I dropped my eyes and looked at the ground. Here it comes.

"I have a young man who feeds the horses in the mornings and turns out the horses who don't live outside, and I have Jodie, who comes in the afternoons after school to clean the turned out horsess' stalls, and then I help her bring them in after she does the water and sweeps the aisles."

I nodded at the ground.

"Until you came along. You came here on Monday and worked with a yearling. Then you came on Tuesday and Wednesday and helped Jodie bring the horses in. Today she waited for you to help her clean stalls. I'm gonna have a talk with her. I don't want that to happen again."

"Okay."

"Now she's gonna be late bringing the horse in because she waited around for you, but I guess if we both help her bring the horse in when she's finished with her work, then we won't be running too late."

I looked up at Craig.

"In the meantime," he said, "go get me the black yearling with the blanket and 2 socks behind. His name is Wisdom." He handed me the rope halter he was wearing over his shoulder.

I looked up at Craig. I wasn't being kicked off the property. I grabbed the rope halter and opened the pasture gate.

On Friday, at the end of the day, Craig walked into the barn as Jodie and I were bringing the last of the horses in. Without saying a word, he handed each of us an envelope. Then he walked into the tackroom.

Jodie tore open her envelope and pulled out a check. "Well, okay," she said, smiling at me. "I thought he might dock my pay since you showed up, but it's the same. I'm happy," she said.

I didn't ask her how much she was paid. I just opened my envelope and peeked in at the check. It was made out to "Ms. L. Madison" and it was more money than I had ever made working at a barn.

6 - THE HORSE SHOW

My mother came back to Aunt Mae's late Saturday evening, pulling a small trailer. I could tell she was exhausted, so I took little Buddy out of her arms. He immediately started crying, but I bounced him a little and he shut up.

My middle brother, Danny, ran up to me and hugged me. Danny was a 6-year-old and had just started school. Now his mother was leaving his father and his world was being turned upside down. I hoped I could help him adjust to our new life.

My older brother, Tommy, was busy unloading the trailer. Tommy was 16 and almost a man. He had a black eye, and I knew he probably got it from our father because he had trouble keeping his mouth shut when our mother and father were fighting. Tommy planned to enlist in the Marine Corps when he graduated from high school. It suited him. He would be successful.

After Buddy fell asleep, I carried him into Aunt Mae's tiny house and laid him on our mother's bed. I put him in the corner of the bed and put the pillows at his side so he wouldn't roll off it. He probably wouldn't hurt himself if he did roll off it because he was a chubby little man.

When I was convinced he would remain asleep, I went out and helped Tommy and Danny unload the trailer. Our mother was in the kitchen with Aunt Mae, preparing dinner and telling Aunt Mae about leaving our father.

"He drank all week, and I was afraid he wouldn't be able to keep his doctor's appointment this morning, but he surprised me. He got up, bathed, shaved, and put some clean clothes on. His brother picked him up at 8:45 that morning, and off they went."

"Were you afraid he would come back and catch you packing up to leave?" Aunt Mae asked her.

"No. I knew he and his brother would hit the bars after their doctor's appointments. I wasn't worried about that. Besides, I had everything all packed up. All the boys and I had to do was load it onto the trailer."

"Mom, where do you want this?" I was carrying Buddy's toy box.

Mother looked at Aunt Mae. "Living room?"

Aunt Mae nodded. I turned to go to the living room, but Mother stopped me. "Layne, did you get the job?"

I turned back around and looked at her. "The check is on your dresser. He made it out to Ms. L. Madison, so you can cash it." I left the room without waiting for a reply. My mother's first name was Laura, but I didn't think Craig knew that.

Danny, Tommy, and I finished unloading the trailer

and put 3 folding chairs at the small kitchen table. I put paper plates in front of the chairs and Mom put a glass of milk beside each plate and a plate of sandwiches in the middle of the table. Then she wiped her hands and sat down on one of the folding chairs. Aunt Mae was already seated, watching us.

When we were all seated, Mother said grace. "Thank you Father for this food. Forgive us our sins and teach us to forgive those who sin against us. Amen."

Aunt Mae snorted but said nothing.

"I'll pray for you tonight, Mae," my mother told her.

Aunt Mae looked at her. "Save it," she said. "Pray for yourself and your young'uns."

Mother did not reply, so I grabbed a ham and cheese sandwich from the plate in the middle of the table and passed around a bag of chips.

"Tommy can work at the dairy after school," Aunt Mae said. "We were gonna hire more help anyway."

"Danny will might have trouble getting a job," my mother said. "Maybe he can cut grass or something."

"I can paint too," Danny said in his quiet voice.

"We will see," Mother said and ran her fingers through Danny's hair.

My mother could work only nights and weekends until Buddy was 3 years old. Then he could go to pre-school. He could go to kindergarten when he turned 5. In the meantime, she would clean houses and offices at night when Buddy was asleep and the rest of us were home to keep an eye on him.

I didn't have to work on Sunday, but I went to the barn anyway. Craig just nodded at me and gave me a rope halter. "Tango is the palomino," he said.

The yearlings were learning fast, and that was a good thing because Craig planned to wean this year's foal crop in October. There were 5 of them and I thought he might want me to work with them. We also had 6 mares due to foal in April and May of the next year. I didn't want to show it, but I was excited about my future at Rivervale.

The week flew by and soon it was Friday. I dropped my bike at the entrance to the barn and went to the tackroom to grab a rope halter. I almost collided with Craig as I walked in.

"Slow down, Layne! The yearlings will wait for you."

"Sorry."

"I won't be here next Friday," he said. "I have a horse show in Omaha, and I'll be leaving around noon on Friday. I'll be back Sunday afternoon or evening. Ron and Jodie will be working Friday, Saturday and Sunday, so you will have plenty of company."

"Omaha, Nebraska? I'm from Lincoln, Nebraska." It was just a few miles away.

"Yep."

"Actually, I was gonna ask you if I could have that

weekend off. I want to go see my father in Lincoln."

"Sure," Craig said. "Maybe you could get out of school early next Friday, help me load up the trailer and ride with me to Omaha. You could catch the bus to Lincoln from there. Just an idea."

"Wow, that's a great idea. But I'm not telling my mother I'm going," I said.

"Suit yourself. The offer's open."

"I'll be here first thing in the morning next Friday. I'll ditch school."

"Okay, but know that I don't approve," Craig smiled at me.

I smiled too. I wondered how many school days he had ditched for horse shows when he was younger.

Mother let me keep fifty dollars each week out of my paycheck. I never had that much money before. Each week, I would put the fifty dollars in my wallet and wonder what to do with it. I never carried a purse. A purse wasn't practical around livestock, so I always carried a man's wallet in my jeans or overalls.

I had plenty of money for my trip to Lincoln, and I was anxious to talk to my father about why he and my mother split up. I was afraid it was my fault. But I didn't want my mother to know I was visiting him. She would be upset with me because I knew she didn't want to go back to Nebraska.

When Friday finally came, I was at the farm by

sunrise and dropped my bike at the side of the barn and out of everyone's way.

Craig was in the tackroom, sorting out tack and getting ready to load the trailer. Three horses were going to the horse show and each had a saddle, a bridle, leg wraps, sheets and hay bags to load. We also had to load enough bedding, grain and hay for three days. I grabbed a wheelbarrow and started filling it with supplies and tossed a pitchfork on top.

"Easy. Don't pile on too much and hurt yourself," Craig said.

I just looked at him and threw another grooming kit on the wheelbarrow.

Once the trailer was loaded with supplies, we pulled Truman out of his stall and started wrapping his legs for the trip.

Craig watched as I grabbed a polo wrap and a bell boot. I placed the end of the wrap on the front of Truman's cannon bone and started going around his leg, wrapping up to his knee, overlapping a half of the wrap's width as I went up, then down, around the fetlock, made a figure eight around the fetlock, then down the pastern and back up. Another figure eight at the fetlock and up the cannon bone, overlapping all the way until I reached the perfect end under Truman's knee where the velcro met itself and closed securely. Then I put the bell boot over his hoof and Craig handed me another polo wrap and bell boot.

"I can see you know what you're doing, so I'll go

get the paperwork and my things loaded in the living quarters. I'll meet you back here in 15 minutes."

"Okay."

I was secretly pleased that Craig trusted me to wrap the horses. It was an important job that had to be done correctly. A loose wrap could spook a horse and cause chaos in the trailer. A tight leg wrap could cause injury and a forgotten bell boot could cause a shoe to be torn off or come loose on a road trip if a horse stumbled and stepped on it or caught it on something.

When Craig returned, we wrapped the last horse's legs together and loaded them on the trailer. Craig said goodbye to Jodie and Ron and we pulled out of the driveway and headed to Nebraska.

We rode in silence. I think Craig was content to drive without conversation and I had a lot going through my mind while watching the scenery on the drive.

I was wondering what I had done to make my father fight with my mother. She probably told him I got fired again, and that started an argument. I just wanted to know. I didn't want to go back to Nebraska because I loved my job at Rivervale, but I wanted to know what happened between my parents. And I planned to give my father some money.

At the show grounds, I set up the stalls with fresh shavings, water and hay, while Craig unloaded the horses. Then he unhitched the trailer and drove me to the bus station in Omaha. A couple of hours later, I was in Lincoln and standing in the living room of what used to be my house.

My father wasn't home. I assumed he was at the bar. If he was, he wouldn't return home until after 3 am when the bars closed.

The house was a mess. I hate housework, but I started to clean. I had a lot of time and nothing to do, so I loaded up the dishwasher and turned it on, straightened up the living room, gathered dirty laundry and scrubbed the toilet and bathtub. I swept the floors and mopped the bathroom, kitchen and hall. Then I vacuumed the living room and bedrooms. After that, it was only 1 am so I took a shower and put on the clean clothes I had packed in my duffle bag. Then I turned on the TV, popped a DVD in it and fell asleep within minutes, sitting on the couch.

My father came home at 4 am. He stumbled in the front door, coughed, and I jumped. I startled him.

"Well," he growled, "lookie whoze here!"

"Hi," I said.

"Humph. Hi y'self," he said. Then he plopped down in a chair and pulled his shoes off. I could smell his feet, mixed with the stench of whiskey.

"I came to talk to you," I said. I didn't know if he heard me. He had his head down, looking at his socks.

Finally, he said, "K."

"Why did you and Mom split up?"

He looked at me with unfocused eyes. "Din split up. She lef."

"Was it because of me?"

He just looked at me for a long time. Then he dropped his eyes."Nah." He pulled a sock off. "I'll tell ya why she lef', he said, waving the sock at me. "She lef' 'cause she wantz mora this," and he grabbed his private parts.

He threw his sock on the floor. "Night," he said, and pushed off the chair and stumbled down the hallway into his bedroom, one sock off, one sock on. I heard the bedroom door slam shut.

I sat on the couch and watched the end of the DVD without seeing it. I felt nothing. Then I got restless and, eventually, my restlessness turned into anger. I had come all this way to talk to my father, and he insulted my mother, and then fell asleep without noticing that I had cleaned up the house for him.

I balled up my fists and went to the TV. I snapped it off and jerked the DVD out of it and threw it on top of the coffee table.

Then I went to my father's bedroom. The stench of whiskey and body odor covered my face when I opened the door. It was almost unbearable. I gasped to breathe as I walked into the room.

My father stirred on the bed and rolled over onto his back. He opened his filmy eyes and looked at me. Then he grabbed me. "Com'ere. I'll show you what women are good for."

He grabbed the waist of my jeans and popped the top button off. Then he tried to un-zip my jeans.

My head exploded. I jerked back and balled up my fists. I slugged him across the face with my right fist and hit him under the chin with my left fist. Then I hit him under his nose with my right fist. Under and upward. I heard his nose crunch. He let go of my jeans and lay still.

Good, I thought. Bastard.

After I slammed the bedroom door, I heard him vomit. I grabbed my overnight bag and stomped to the front door. I slammed it as I left.

I walked all the way back to the bus station. I was still angry when I got there, but I had to wait until 5am for the next bus to Omaha and it gave me time to cool down.

I got to Omaha a few minutes after 6 and got a ride to the show grounds by 7. Craig was filling hay bags when I walked up.

"Short trip?" he said.

"He wasn't home."

"I have a class at 8. Truman. You can wrap his legs."

I spent the weekend at the horse show, and the lie I told my mother became the truth.

7 - MY DECISION

That weekend was when I decided I wanted to be a dressage trainer with my own farm. Before that weekend I always thought I would become some kind of successful somebody, make a lot of money and take care of my parents. But, after that weekend, I decided to follow my dreams and become a dressage trainer, like Craig, with my own farm.

I was only fourteen, but I could do all the ground work, start a horse under saddle, and make him safe for Craig to train. I had to convince Craig to train me so I could be successful, like him. That meant I had to take lessons and start showing in dressage.

Craig was showing 3 horses that weekend and I helped him every step of the way. It was my goal to become indispensable. I fed the horses, cleaned their stalls, wrapped their legs, tacked them up and lunged them if they needed it.

After their classes, I untacked them, cooled them out, and put them in their stalls with hay and fresh water. If they were finished showing for the day, I bathed them, dried them as much as possible, then put them in their stalls with a cooler and a full hay bag. When they were completely dry, I pulled the cooler off and put a sheet on them for the night. At the end of the day, I fed them again, filled their hay bags and topped off their water. If their braids needed touching up or re-braiding, I did that too.

Craig went for dinner with another trainer and his wife, and I thought, someday that will be me. I was surprised when he brought me a carry-out from the restaurant for my dinner.

"Thanks," I said. "I'll eat it when I finish Truman's braids. Evidently, he had a big itch after winning that class!"

That's when Craig finally asked me, "Where did you learn all the groundwork, how to start a horse and how to braid?" he asked.

I looked at him. I had gotten taller, and I could almost look him straight in the eyes, especially when standing on the braiding stool. "I've been working with horses since I was 10. I started working when I was 8 years old, but it was with cows. When I was 9, the farm I worked at bought a few horses for the owner's family, but they were rank. I loved being around them. So the owner said I could ride them if I got all my work done."

Craig smiled and nodded. I'm sure he saw, in his mind, what happened.

"I got all my work done in half the time it took before so I could work with the horses. I got bucked off, run away with, and trampled too. But I knew animals don't act that way for no reason, so I found out what made them afraid or angry and tried to fix it. The horses got quieter and settled down eventually, and I decided then that I wanted to work with horses the rest of my life."

Craig was still smiling but said nothing. When he started to walk away, I decided it was time to ask him to teach me dressage.

"Craig!" I said a little sharply. He jumped a little, stopped walking, and turned around to face me.

I was as surprised as he was at the tone my of voice. "I want you to teach me dressage. I want lessons and I want to show." I took a deep breath. I had probably blown it.

Craig just smiled and nodded. Then he walked away.

I exhaled. I hadn't blown it.

Craig had his gold medal. He had paid his dues and climbed the ladder. He was successful. He had his own farm, and he bred warmblood Appaloosa horses. Who would be better to teach me the ropes? Suddenly it seemed that fate had placed me in the perfect spot to pursue my dreams, and my father being an asshole freed me to pursue them.

Craig was showing in 6 classes the following day. I stood by the warm-up ring, holding his coat and a rag to wipe his boots. I watched him warm-up the horses and noted how he let them stretch their necks forward and move in long, loose strides. They reached down with each stride, but their noses never came behind their ears. That meant they were using their backs and hind legs correctly.

After they stretched and were moving forward, he asked them to move sideways. Their rhythm never changed as they moved across the ring. When he asked them to canter, they moved effortlessly into canter and kept a light connection to his hand.

When Craig finished the warm-up, he walked the horse through the gate of the warm-up ring and reached for his coat. I handed it to him and cleaned the dust off his boots with a towel. Then I wiped the horse's mouth and nose with the clean side of the towel, and took the leg wraps off. When Craig headed to the show ring, I followed and watched his performance.

In the past, I had learned almost everything I knew from watching. But I wanted to learn faster now. That's why I had to have lessons from Craig. I would still watch everything he and other good riders did, but lessons would speed up my learning curve. I didn't have any time to waste.

8 - LIFE GOES ON

I got home Sunday evening. It was almost dark when I dumped my bicycle by the front porch and stumbled up the steps. I threw my duffel bag under the couch and went into the kitchen.

Mom had left a sandwich and chips for me, and I collapsed at the table to eat it. She must have heard me because she came into the kitchen, opened the refrigerator and took out a jug of milk. She poured me a glass full and sat down.

"How was the horse show?" she said.

I was hungry and as tired, but her question filled me with energy.

"It was great! Craig is amazing, and I learned so much! I want to be a dressage trainer. I want to have my own farm."

Mother smiled and patted my arm. "That's great, honey. Do you have any homework?"

"No," I lied. I would do it before class started tomorrow morning.

"Okay, sweetie. I'm beat. I'm going to bed. The boys have had a long day and they're all asleep. We will see you in the morning."

I finished eating and put my plate in the sink. I was beat too and decided not to take a shower. Maybe I would take one tomorrow morning.

But when the morning came, I was wide awake and in a hurry. The shower could wait. I got dressed in a clean t-shirt and almost clean jeans and grabbed my books, threw them in the basket on my bike and headed for school. When I got there, I threw my bike into the bike rack and ran inside to do the weekend's homework.

I made it through the day somehow and headed to the farm after school. Craig was showing Yahoo, one of his long yearlings, which means he was soon to be a 2-year-old, to a couple of women when I entered the barn. They walked around the beautifully marked Appaloosa warmblood colt and looked at his strong, straight legs and his short back.

Yahoo arched his neck proudly and watched them walk around him. He stood perfectly still until Craig asked him to walk forward, turned him and walked him back to the women. Then Craig asked him to trot forward and back for them.

Craig's long legs moved as effortlessly as the colt's. The women smiled and whispered to each other. Craig untied the rope halter and slipped it off Yahoo's head. The colt stood perfectly still.

Craig asked the women to walk with him and took them to the center of the arena. Then he picked up a lunge whip and, signalling Yahoo, he asked him to walk off, trot and then canter around the arena. Yahoo moved even more beautifully free than he had in-hand. I knew that was because, in-hand, he had to match his stride to the handler's stride. When he went under saddle in the future, he would, if the rider was allowed it, show off his beautiful strides.

The ladies whispered to each other again.

I watched them from behind the arena gate, and Yahoo saw me as he floated by. When Craig was finished lunging him, I called Yahoo over to me.

Yahoo trotted to the gate and stuck his nose over it. I rubbed his nose. "Good boy," I said.

Craig saw me then. "Layne, bring Yahoo here, please."

I opened the gate and touched Yahoo's neck. "Come," I said, and Yahoo followed me. I walked toward Craig and the women. I stopped a few feet from them and Yahoo stopped beside me.

Craig walked up to us and stood on the left side of the colt with his back to the women. He bent over, wove his fingers together, and looked at me. I understood and put my left knee in the cup he had made with his hands, and Craig lifted me up onto Yahoo's back. Then he turned to face the women.

Yahoo stood still beside Craig while I rubbed his neck and mane. Craig walked toward them, and Yahoo and I followed him. We stopped 3 feet from the ladies. I laid down on Yahoo's back and slid backwards toward his rump, then off his backside to the arena footing, holding Yahoo's tail as I slid off him. Then I patted his side and said, "Good boy."

"Well," the woman with long blond hair said, "I don't think he will be hard to saddle train! Can we go somewhere and talk?" she asked Craig.

Craig handed me the rope halter, and I put it on Yahoo and led him out to the pasture. He was probably sold. I would miss him, but all the yearlings were for sale. That's why Craig bred them.

I was looking forward to the next year's foal crop, and I was hoping to stay at the barn overnight to see the foals born. Most mares foaled at night or in the wee hours of the morning, Craig told me. I was hoping I could spend a few nights at the barn during foaling season.

When I got home that afternoon, Mom was waiting for me. She was sitting on the porch, watching me as I propped my bike against the side of the house and walked slowly up the stairs. I had never seen my mother sitting down, except to eat a quick meal. She was always in motion, going here and there. Always moving and working.

Buddy was somewhere in the house, crying. I could hear him struggling to breathe, which meant he had been crying for a while.

"I'll go get Buddy," I said to her.

"No. Stay. Sit down," my mother said in a strained voice.

I sat in the folding chair by her side and waited. I knew I was in trouble, and I wondered what I had done.

Finally, she spoke, "Your father is dead." She never looked at me. She was staring at the road in front of Aunt Mae's house.

"The neighbor found him this morning. Evidently, he had been drinking, got into a fight, and came home and fell asleep on his bed. He vomited and suffocated himself. It's called 'death by aspiration,' they said.

I stopped breathing and gripped the arms of my chair.

"A couple of cops came here this morning. They had been notified by the authorities in Lincoln and came to tell me."

I had killed my father.

I had killed him with my bare hands.

I loosened my grip on the chair and put my hands in my lap. I looked down at my 14-year-old hands. I had killed my father. How was that possible? I had been angry. Very angry.

I had killed him.

My mother was talking, but I didn't hear her. I didn't hear Buddy crying, either. I didn't hear anything but the sound of blood roaring in my ears. I jumped up and ran to the edge of the porch and threw up. My whole body wretched, and I coughed.

My mother stood up and walked over to me. She rubbed my back. "It's okay, Layne. It will be okay," she said.

How could it ever be okay? I had killed him. I had killed my father.

When Aunt Mae and Tommy came home from their jobs at the dairy farm, my mother had to tell them, too. I wondered how Danny would take it. He loved his father more than the rest of us.

I held Buddy and bounced him while she talked to Aunt Mae and the two boys.

Tommy didn't say a word, but Danny cried and hugged Mom. She held him and rubbed his back, then pushed him away. "Be a big boy now. I need you to be strong."

Danny nodded and rubbed his eyes with his fists.

Aunt Mae was sitting on the porch watching Mom. When Mom finished talking to the boys, she sighed and rubbed her hands together. They made a rough sound, like sandpaper on wood. Then she slapped her hands on her knees and said, "I'm gonna go fry up some burgers and taters."

I guess that was the day my attitude toward my brothers changed. I felt alone, powerful and afraid of myself. I felt removed from Danny. I couldn't laugh at his antics anymore. He looked just like my father. Tommy had always been strong and silent, and I felt most comfortable around him. Buddy was just a baby, but his crying made me nervous.

Not that I had a lot of time to spend with the boys. Between school, work and lessons at Rivervale and helping Aunt Mae and Mom around the house, I found time to sleep and that was about it.

But no matter how I felt about it, life went on. Mother returned to Lincoln and made arrangements for our father's funeral. She didn't ask us to go back for the funeral, and that was a relief. She sorted through paperwork, and filed for some kind of support for Danny, Buddy and me as minor children. She got a little life insurance money too. When she returned to Nisland, she had the paperwork for Tommy to join the Marines when he turned seventeen.

So, our father's death reaped some benefits for her and the boys. I got a big knot in my gut that I would carry inside me for years to come, and I had a new respect for the power of my anger.

9 - MARLBORO

Time passed, and the foals were due. I wanted so much to see them born that I finally got up the courage to ask Craig if I could stay at the barn during foaling season.

There was an observation room attached to the arena, and it had a storage room in it. Next to the storage room was a bathroom with a shower. I could sleep in the storage room and take a shower before going to school. No one would even know I was there unless they came around late at night and saw my bike parked on the side of the barn. I really didn't think Craig would let me stay there, and I was afraid to ask.

But when Gypsy bagged up and Craig said she would foal in a day or two, and I asked him.

To my surprise, he said yes. He nodded and said, "Yeah. I wouldn't mind that at all. We could take turns checking on her."

He didn't ask me where I planned to stay, but I guess he had that all figured out because there was a folding cot in the storage room and a couple of bath towels in the bathroom the next day.

"You take the hours from 10 to 2, and I will check on Gypsy 3 to 7. After 7, Ron will be in the barn and he will keep an eye on Gypsy," Craig said.

"Great. I'm really looking forward to this," I said.

"Well, you might miss it all," Craig said. "Mares usually foal during the middle of the night, when the barn is quiet. My mares usually foal around 3 am, so you might miss everything."

I stuck my lower lip out and balled up my fists. "You better wake me up, then! If I'm sleeping and I miss everything, I'm gonna be mad!"

Craig's eyes got round and, laughing, he said, "Take it easy! I'll wake you up. No problem."

I relaxed and realized I might have scared Craig a little. I scared myself. That was when I knew I had to get a handle on my emotions. I couldn't let people know what I was feeling all the time.

I consciously relaxed my body, unclenched my fists and managed to smile. "Thanks. I really appreciate it."

Craig nodded and smiled. "This arrangement will be better than me running out to the barn every couple of hours, like I've always done in the past," he said.

I had to clear everything with my mother and Aunt Mae. Fortunately, Aunt Mae knew how tiring the birthing season could be and convinced my mother that I would probably be happy to come home after a few sleepless nights in the barn. "Let her try it this weekend, sis. She'll be home Sunday night, I bet."

It was Friday night, and I didn't have to go to school the next morning. I looked at my mother, willing her to say yes.

"Okay," my mother said. "Let's see how tired you are Monday morning when you have to get up and go to school."

I went to the barn early Saturday morning. I found Craig in the broodmare barn, wrapping Gypsy's tail. He had it braided and folded up onto her tail bone and he was wrapping it up in vet wrap. "Not too tight," he told me. "We don't want to cut off the circulation. We just want to keep it out of the way and clean."

I nodded and watched him finish up.

"I think she's really close to foaling," he said. "She started dripping milk this morning. Not a lot, and that's good. The foal needs the colostrum."

"What's colostrum?"

"It's a mare's first milk. It's loaded with antibodies to make the foal's immune system strong. It stimulates his first poop and it gives him gut microbes too so he can digest hay and grain when he gets his first teeth."

Gypsy's water broke that night. I was sitting on the aisle floor, leaned against her stall door and nodding off, when I heard her pee. At first, I thought she was just peeing. A big pee. A very big pee.

My eyes flew open, and I sat up. That was her water breaking and it was a flood, just like Craig said.

I jumped up, ran to the house and pounded on Craig's door. No answer. I tried again and eventually heard him yell, "Coming!" from the back of the house.

"Gypsy's water broke," I told him through the screen when he came to the door dressed in jeans and a white t-shirt. Craig reached for his boots and hopped on one leg, pulling them on. Then he jerked the door open, almost knocking me down, and we ran to the barn.

When we got there, two feet were sticking out of Gypsy's hind end.

I gasped.

"Perfect," Craig said.

But the mare was restless. She was walking around and around in her stall. Every now and then, she would bump the foal's protruding legs against the wall.

That really worried me. We were still standing outside the stall. I wanted to go in and do something, but I had no idea what. "Is she hurting the foal?" I asked Craig.

"No. See the little pads on the foal's feet? They are cushions. They protect the mare's uterus when the baby is inside her, and they will fall off after he's born."

"Yeah," I said, "but they're not hitting the walls. His legs are."

"Don't worry. He's pretty flexible right now, and she's probably using the wall on purpose to re-position him in some way."

I breathed a sigh of relief, but my hands were sweating. I wanted to walk behind the mare and hold the foal's legs away from the wall, but I restrained myself. Craig was wise. He had been through this many times.

The mare continued to walk in circles in her stall. Even though her stall was bigger than a normal horse's stall, she kept turning and bumping up against the wall. "Why is she walking around so much? Is everything okay?"

"Yes. She will lay down in a minute. Gypsy's had a few foals. She knows what she's doing," Craig reassured me. "Just watch her. I'm glad she was first this year. You'll learn a lot from her."

Sure enough, soon Gypsy laid down again. And pushed. Craig said, "Not every mare will let you in the stall, but be quiet, move slowly and watch me." Then he opened the stall door and entered, leaving the door open for me to follow. I crept in after him and slid the stall door shut.

Gypsy pushed again and the colt's nose emerged from her vulva. I watched as Craig knelt down behind the mare and put his hands around the foal's protruding legs.

He turned to me as I knelt beside him. "Never pull a foal," he told me. "You can pull a cow, but you still have to be careful to not damage the cow's uterus. With a mare, you just hold the feet and wait until she pushes. All you want to do is prevent the foal from slipping back into the womb."

I nodded, breathless and stared at Craig's hands..

"Now is the hardest part for the mare. She has to pass the shoulders through the birth canal. She might rest after that. So we need to clear the placenta and mucus from the foal's nose to make sure he can breathe. Then we wait. After she passes the shoulders, the rest is easy. The mare usually gets up then. She will turn around, tearing the placenta away from the foal and dragging it behind herself. Next, she will start licking the foal. That's when you want to tie up the placenta to keep it from dragging in the bedding. When she releases the placenta, and it drops into the stall, put it in a bucket and save it for me to examine so I can make sure all of it was expelled. A retained placenta, or even a partially retained placenta, will make a mare very sick. Then we're in trouble."

My mouth was open, taking in everything Craig was telling me.

Fortunately, the foaling went perfectly, as Craig predicted. Gypsy released the placenta and I grabbed it and put it in the bucket sitting outside the stall door.

The foal was still wet and shivering a little. "That's not always the case, but a little shivering is normal," Craig said. A few minutes later, the foal tried to stand. After a few heart-wrenching falls, he was standing on his long, bony legs, reaching under the mare to nurse.

Craig turned to me and smiled, "Excellent," he said. "We can leave now. See you in the morning."

I nodded and stumbled out of the stall behind Craig. I don't remember going into the storage room and falling onto the cot, but I woke to my alarm at 6 am and ran to Gypsy's stall to see the foal before grabbing my bicycle and going to school.

Hannah and Winsome were due to foal next. It was a toss-up which would foal first, but Hannah showed signs on Wednesday, and I kept a close watch on her that night. I was walking back from my hourly check on Hannah when I heard a whinny coming from Winsome's stall. Winsome wasn't a friendly mare, and I was surprised that she whinnied at me.

I peeked in her stall and, even though she wasn't dripping first milk, something told me she was going to foal soon. She stood patiently while I wrapped her tail, as I had seen Craig do with Gypsy. Then I brushed her and added a little more straw to her stall. It seemed that she didn't want me to leave, so I slid down and sat in the corner of her stall. Winsome lowered her head and blew on me.

"You're fine," I said. Craig had told me this was Winsome's first foal, so she was probably confused and a little spooked by the changes taking place inside her.

Then I heard Hannah lay down in her stall. I got up and left Winsome's stall to check on Hannah. Winsome watched me leave and pawed a little at her bedding.

Hannah's water broke as soon as I opened her stall door. She lay in the stall, tail unwrapped and wet. I quickly grabbed the tail wrap I had left outside her stall and did my best to wrap up the wet, straw clogged mess. Within minutes, feet appeared in her vulva and a red and white nose followed. Hannah nickered.

"Good girl," I said, breathless.

A couple of minutes later, her foal was born, and Hannah was up, placenta dragging in the stall. She started to lick her foal, and it bobbed its head. I quickly cleaned out its nostrils and listened to it breathe. Then I went to Hannah and tied her placenta in a knot. It immediately fell to the ground, so I gathered it up and put it in a bucket outside the stall for Craig to examine. I was not sure if it was all there, but Craig would know.

I didn't have time to go get Craig, though.

Winsome banged on her stall wall and went down.

I left Hannah's stall before the foal was nursing, but Winsome was down and I had to check on her. I didn't have time to even think about getting Craig.

And, sure enough, Winsome was having her foal. She grunted, and I stroked her shoulder. "It's okay. You can do this," I told her.

But she wasn't having an easy time of it. Her water hadn't broken, and I started to worry. Should I leave and go get Craig? Winsome thumped her head on the bedding, and I decided to stay with her a little longer.

Then her water broke. I relaxed a little and waited. Winsome grunted again, but nothing happened. I was starting to panic. Should I go get Craig? I knew we had only a half hour for the foal to be born once the water broke. Then I saw a hoof. Just one. There should be two, but Winsome got up, and the hoof disappeared inside her. I panicked, thinking I should have grabbed it.

Then she walked around the stall, as Gypsy had done, and I looked at my watch. Five minutes. Don't panic. Stay calm. Winsome stood in the corner of the stall and looked at me.

"Please lay down," I begged her.

But she just looked at me. "I have to leave," I told her. "I have to get Craig."

I turned to leave and opened the stall door. Winsome laid down again, and I saw two feet peeking out of her vulva. I blew out a sigh of relief, knelt down and held the foal's feet and waited. And waited. Nothing happened.

I was panicking again. I decided I really had to go get Craig when she groaned, and a dark brown nose appeared on top of the legs. I gripped both legs with my left hand and tore open the placenta and cleaned out the foal's nostrils with my right hand.

I remembered it was her first foal, and I knew she would need help, but I didn't know what to do. Calm down, I told myself. I took hold of the slippery legs with both hands and waited.

Winsome dropped her head in the bedding. It sounded like she was asleep. I panicked and took my right hand off the foal's leg and smacked her. "Get busy!" I yelled.

Winsome's head popped up, and I smacked her again. She contracted her muscles, and the foal slid out at my knees.

"Yes!" I breathed, and cleared the placenta from

the foal's body. I took a rag from my jeans and wiped out its nostrils again because I realized that I hadn't heard it breathe yet. Then foal coughed and took its first noisy breath. I sat back and smiled.

Then I looked at Winsome. She was laying in the straw and not moving. I jumped up and ran to her head. I put my hand in front of her nose. She was breathing, but it looked like she was sleeping. I slapped her on her neck. Winsome popped her head up and looked at me. Then I grabbed her head and pushed it around to her side. "Look at what you did! Look!"

Winsome looked at the foal and did not move. Then she nickered. I waited and wondered what I should do next, but Winsome got to her feet and shook her whole body. The placenta dropped to the ground, and I grabbed it and put it in the bucket outside her stall door.

Winsome went to her foal and smelled him. Then she started licking him. He bobbed his head and soon got to his feet without falling. I collapsed in the straw and wondered if I had enough energy to go get Craig.

Two more foals were born within the month, and I thought I could handle any foaling until Savannah had her foal. She wouldn't let him nurse. She wouldn't even let him get near her. She kept moving away and flicking her tail.

"Put a halter on her and hold her," Craig said. "It's her first foal, so she's probably confused or maybe her bag is sensitive."

So I held her. Then Craig moved the foal closer to her. He stretched his nose toward her bag and she tried to kick him.

We tried twice more, but Savannah got more irritated each time.

"She's a first-time mare," Craig said. "Let's give her some time and try again in an hour."

I nodded and watched as the foal collapsed in a corner of the stall and fell asleep. An hour later, the foal was up and looking at the mare, but afraid to approach her. I held the mare again and Craig brought the foal up to her. She immediately swung her backside away from the foal. Craig tried again, but the mare swung her backside away again and kicked the wall.

Craig let the foal wobble away from Savannah and collapse again in the corner of the stall. Then he turned to me. "I'm going to get a bottle. Don't take the halter off. Just hold her and I'll be back in a few minutes."

"Okay." I was exhausted and almost in tears.

Craig returned and approached Savannah. He stretched his body toward her, with his left hand holding the bottle and resting on her back. He touched her bag with his right hand. Savannah flicked her tail. Then he touched her nipple and she lifted her leg.

I held my breath, ready to bolt.

"Watch how I milk the mare," he said, "because we might have to do this for a day or two."

"Okay."

Craig pulled on Savannah's nipple and a drop of clear liquid came out. She sighed and relaxed her leg. Then Craig dropped his left hand and moved closer. He bent his tall frame and, holding the bottle under her nipple, he milked the mare. Then he straightened his body, moving slowly and stroked her on the rump.

"Don't try this," he said. "She knows me, but I'm not sure how she will act with anyone else. I don't want anyone getting hurst. I just want you to know how it's done."

I let out the breath I was holding and nodded.

Then Craig approached the foal, who was watching from the corner. He lifted the foals head and rubbed the nipple of the bottle against his muzzle, which opened. Then he rubbed the nipple on his gums. The foal stuck out his tongue and licked his gums. Then he latched onto the bottle and sucked greedily.

Craig looked at me. "Don't cry," he said. "It will be okay."

I swallowed hard and nodded.

We tried two hours later to get Savannah to nurse the foal, but she refused to let him near her.

Finally, Craig called the vet.

The vet asked to see the placenta and then he gave Savannah a dose of calcium and watched our efforts to unite the mare and her foal. But Savannah wanted nothing to do with the strange looking creature in her stall.

The vet shook his head. "Well, keep trying. Milk her if she remains uncooperative." He grabbed his bag and left saying, "Good luck."

After the vet left, Craig looked at me and said, "I won't be breeding this mare again. It looks like we have an orphan on our hands."

"But he's not an orphan. The mare's still here," I said.

"He's an orphan, alright," Craig said. "She won't feed him, and we can't trust her with him. As he gets stronger and more rambunctious, she might hurt him. I doubt she will ever accept him. We have to separate them and hand-raise him. Yep, we have an orphan on our hands."

"Oh."

"I will have to bottle feed him until I can find a surrogate mare or a milking goat. Once he can eat hay and grain we have to watch his growth plates," Craig said.

"What are growth plates?"

"Horses' joints grow in stages," he explained. "They grow from the ground up. If a foal eas too much grain, or gets too much protein from rich hay or lush grass, their joints swell or their ligaments and tendons out-grow their bones. So getting enough exercise and the proper amount of food will be important. We have to keep an eye on him."

"Okay." I was learning a lot.

"And the other important thing to watch is his

behavior," Craig said.

"What do you mean?"

"Orphan foals don't know how to be a horse," he said. "Tthey don't have the mare to discipline and guide them, so they tend to be too pushy or timid. They need another horse or person, like a surrogate mare, to teach themm how to be a horse."

"Oh." I didn't think Craig had a surrogate mare.

"Or someone to act like a mare." He was looking at me.

"Okay. I'll do it, but I don't know what to do."

"Yes, you do," Craig said. "Just teach him manners and teach him not to be afraid of new things. After all, everything is new to a baby."

"Okay. I can do that."

"I know you can. Ron and I will milk the mare and feed him when you're not here. The time will go fast, you'll see. He will have his baby teeth in no time."

Craig looked at me. I realized he was looking for a reply. "Okay. I can do it."

"Then you get to name him."

"Well, that might be hard. I'll have to think about it," I said.

"Take your time," Craig said. "And go get some rest. You look exhausted."

I looked at the foal, sleeping in the corner of the stall. "Will he be okay?"

"I'll stay here until Ron gets here," Craig said. "I'll have to milk the mare then. Go get some rest."

"Okay. Are you sure? I can skip school..."

"Go!" Craig said sternly and laughed when I jumped.

I pretended to punch him on the way out of the stall and Craig laughed again.

On the second day after they were born, Craig and I would imprint the new foals, touching them all over their body. Then we picked them up, put a halter on them, and handled their feet. We would lead the foal away from the mare and walk him around.

Well, that was easy with this foal. We basically took the place of the mare. He let us handle him with no problem, and we could lead him anywhere.

The real problem wasn't that his mother was mean to him. She just wouldn't nurse him, and she didn't want him near her, so we separated them after trying on the second day. I spent as much time with him as possible and slept in the barn with the foal until Craig got him a goat. The goat was a bit of a pain, jumping up and climbing on everything, but she let the foal nurse and kept him company when I couldn't be there.

I named him Marlboro. It was a strong name, and I always pictured the Marlboro man as a loner, like this little guy.

With Craig's permission, I turned Marlboro out with the yearlings so he could have a bit of a social life and grow up like a horse should.

There were a couple of boss horses in the small band of yearlings, but Marlboro was smart enough to stay away from them most of the time. Sometimes he got a too close to one of them and got his butt kicked. But he was quick and never got more than a minor scrape or a bite. It taught him some respect, and I thought that was a good thing. The goat stayed with him, but didn't protect him, so Marlboro had to learn who was the boss and be respectful.

When I went to see him in the pasture, he would follow me around, so he was easy to catch and bring into the stall at night. Craig didn't want to leave him outside with the yearlings overnight, so Marlboro and the goat came inside at night. I usually wound up sleeping in the stall with them whenever I could stay over at the farm.

When Marlboro was 6 months old, Craig decided to sell him. "A lady came today and offered to buy Marlboro," he told me.

I gasped. "No! I want him!" My fists were balled up and I could feel my face turning red.

Craig looked at me, surprised.

I sucked in some air and tried to calm down. "Let me buy him. I'll train him. He won't be a burden to you. Please? I'll pay whatever you want."

"It's not a question of money," Craig said. "We can talk about it later."

"Let me buy him. Schools out and I have a lot of time. I can pay you with extra work. I just need to give my mother rent money. Please let me buy him?" Tears were welling up in my eyes by then, but I still had my hands in balled up in fists.

Craig held up his hands. "We can talk later," he said.

Later never came. We never talked, but I worked with Marlboro each day and took my lessons every week. When we went to horse shows, I braided all the horses and cleaned all the stalls. I never asked for more money and Craig never increased my pay, but he also never offered to sell Marlboro to anyone after that.

When Marlboro was a yearling, he went into the yearling pasture full time, and I saw less of him then. "Let him grow up," Craig said. "He needs to be a horse, not your pet puppy."

It was hard to let him go, but I knew Craig was right.

My lessons were going well. I was able to show with Craig and I had climbed a level that year. When the last horse show of the season rolled around, I was beginning to show at first level and qualified for the regional finals at training level.

Regionals that year were held in Iowa on the weekend of my 15th birthday. I didn't tell Craig it was my birthday, but I guess he knew somehow.

He walked up to me with an envelope in his hand.

"Happy birthday. Better put that away in a safe place before we leave for Regionals," he said.

I took it and stuffed it in my overalls. "Thanks," I thought it was just my weekly paycheck.

"Maybe you'd better open it," Craig said.

"Oh."

I pulled the envelope out of my overalls and opened it. Inside was my paycheck, and behind it was a folded parchment paper. I took it out and unfolded it. It was Marlboro's registration papers. With my name on it as owner. I was speechless.

My mouth fell open, and I looked at Craig.

He reached out with his right hand and gently closed my mouth. "You earned it," he said.

10 - HUSBAND HUNTING

I was training at Prix St. George and showing at third level on one of Craig's horses by the time I turned 17 and graduated from high school.

After graduating from high school, I started working full time at Rivervale Farm. I had earned my bronze medal and Craig allowed me to teach a little. I liked teaching beginners and training level, but I preferred working with horses to teaching.

And I had another job. I was looking for a husband. I realized a husband was the only way I could afford to buy my own farm, but he had to be the right man. He had to be a good earner, focused on me, and easily manipulated.

I had started dating after graduating from high school. I didn't have time to date while I was in high school, and I didn't have any interest in the boys there, anyway. I knew I would have to marry well if I wanted to fulfil my dream of owning a farm. Horse farms like I wanted weren't cheap, and I wanted the best money could buy. So, I had to be smart and marry the right man.

Mother wanted me to go to college, but I told her I didn't need a college degree to work with horses. "The degree I want is Grand Prix," I told her. "It takes a lot longer to get than a college degree, so I need to keep going until I earn my gold medal. Then, with the right credentials, I can teach and train and make a pretty good living. I just need to work hard and get a farm."

My mother blinked, but didn't argue. It wouldn't have done her any good. I knew what I wanted and what it took to get it.

But the one thing I couldn't figure out was how to get enough money to buy what I needed. Horse farms were expensive. I figured that, by the time I could save enough money on my own to get a farm, I would be ready to retire. I would have to make another plan.

I had only a few options. I could work my ass off for other people and never have my own farm, or I could marry money. That was about it.

Fortunately, I grew into an attractive woman. The long hours of physical work had made my body strong, so that was an asset. I had auburn hair and green eyes, and I looked pretty good, even without makeup.

But my possibilities were few. I reluctantly started dating the local veterinarian. I met him when I was still in high school, and working at Rivervale. I always knew he was interested. But I wondered if I could get beyond his glasses and his know-it-all attitude. After our first date, I decided that I would rather kill him than marry him. Besides, I couldn't imagine kissing him or anything else that might be required. So I just ignored him for a while.

That didn't last long. No other options appeared at

the farm, and I couldn't take time off to manhunt, so my choices, at the time, were limited to him.

He was a regular visitor to the farm for spring shots, Coggins tests and minor injuries, but he was a predator. I didn't know it before I dated him, but it became evident on our first date. He took me to dinner at Rivervale's only restaurant and then he tried to kiss me when went out to his truck. I pushed him away.

"Hey, what's the problem?" he said, laughing.

"Your behavior," I said.

"Come on now. Give me a chance!"

"You had your chance. You blew it," I replied and walked home. He didn't know it, but he had just been spared an early death.

I kept looking. A young farrier showed some interest in me, but I knew he liked to party with his friends, and he would never make enough money to buy the farm I wanted. Also, he was a good-looking fellow, and probably wouldn't be faithful. I'd have to kill him, too.

Whoever I dated and decided to marry would have to be faithful and hard-working. The opposite of my father. Then I met Bill.

Bill was a construction worker who came with a crew to enlarge Craig's indoor arena. Craig wanted more room to free-jump his horses and to build a bigger observation room. Bill was the crew foreman, and I was attracted to him right away. He seemed like a serious guy, and I liked that too.

At first, Bill didn't notice me. When I got close enough to see that he didn't have a wedding band, I stumbled and fell up against him.

"Oh! I'm sorry. Excuse me," I said, but fell over enough that he had to catch me.

When he picked me up, I brushed up against him and looked into his eyes. That's all it took. I felt a jolt of electricity jump from him to me and a connection was made. Bill asked me to go to dinner with him that afternoon.

The job for Craig was supposed to take 10 days, but Bill's crew was delayed by a big snowstorm, and it took them 2 weeks, long enough for Bill to fall in love with me and for me to size him up as the man who could make all my dreams come true.

I was out of high school by then and working full time for Craig. I spent every evening with Bill. Not all night, of course. I had him drop me off at night at Aunt Mae's house and pick me up each morning. We had breakfast together and then went to the farm.

At the end of the two weeks, Bill had to leave and return to Michigan for another job. But Bill was in love with me, and I knew he was the one. When he asked me to marry him, I said I couldn't.

"Why? You said you loved me."

"I do," I replied, "but I can't marry you. I have to work hard and save my money so I can buy property and build a barn. I can't get married and have children who will take up all my time and money."

Bill sighed and dropped his head. Then he straightened up and looked me. "I can build you a barn," he said.

"Really? You would do that for me?"

"Yes, but I want children."

"I can do that," I said. But I had no intention of doing that.

"Then let's get married," he said. "We can pick out a ring tonight and set a date."

"Whoa, cowboy, you are leaving town tomorrow, right?"

"Yeah, but you can come with me."

"I can't. I have Marlboro, and I have my job."

Bill dropped his head and rubbed his hands together. "Let's think about this," he said. "If we both get a job in the same area, and in a big enough area to keep me busy, it would work."

I nodded. "That would work."

"Okay. My parents live in Detroit. That's a big place. It's surrounded by other towns. Ann Arbor, Grosse Pointe, Port Huron and all sorts of small towns and rural areas. Maybe you could find a job in at a farm around Detroit or Port Huron."

"That would work," I said again.

So, I accepted his ring and posted an ad on Facebook, looking for a job training dressage horses in the Detroit/Port Huron area. Bonnie was the first to reply to my ad, and I accepted her offer immediately.

Bill made the arrangements, and we moved to

Michigan and brought Marlboro with us. We got married at a clerk's office in Port Huron.

"I don't want to waste money on a big wedding," I told him.

Bill never questioned my lack of interest in sex before we got married. I told him I was a virgin, and that was that. After we got married, he was patient and tried to teach me how to enjoy sex, but I never did. The first time we made what most people call love, I call it animal acts, it hurt. I bled and cried. Bill was patient and didn't try again for 2 weeks.

Two weeks later, I didn't bleed, but I didn't relax either. "It will take time," Bill said.

"How much time?"

"I don't know."

I never enjoyed sex. I dreaded it and thought it was unclean.

Bill thought I was being a bitch. "What's wrong with you?" he yelled at me, eventually.

"Nothing's wrong with me. I just don't like grunting and sweating like an animal. It's nasty, and I feel gross when we do it."

"You're impossible," Bill yelled and marched out of the bedroom, slamming the door. He slept on the couch that night.

But it wasn't until he found my birth control pills that he really lost it.

"What are these?" he yelled, shaking the container in my face.

"Birth control pills," I said.

"Why? I want children," he yelled.

"Well, I don't. Not right now, anyway. I want a farm first," I said, trying to calm him.

"There won't be a farm!" Bill yelled at me. "I won't finance the rest of my life and work my ass off so you can have a farm. No way!"

Bill growled and threw the pills at me. I guess I knew my marriage was over then. I couldn't live with constant fighting. I would wind up killing him.

Fortunately, I had a new plan. But my plan would take a while. In the meantime, I had to placate Bill, so I told him I needed to get a second job so we could save money for our future.

I got a job at a strip club.

X-odus was located in Detroit near 7 Mile Road. The owner's daughter leased a horse at Bonnie's barn and took weekly riding lessons with her. I struck up a conversation with her after one of her lessons.

"Hey, Deanna! Good ride today! Will you be showing with Bonnie next year?"

"I hope so. Your name's Layne, right?"

"Yep. I'm the assistant trainer. Glad to meet you." I offered her my right hand and we shook.

"You too. I've watched you ride. You're good."

"Thanks. I work hard at it. But it's expensive and I hope to get more work soon." I knew her dad owned a bar. I was fishing.

"Well, if you're looking for part time work, you could always dance at my dad's bar. He doesn't pay much, but you can get lots of tips."

"Wow. That sounds great. I'll go see your dad this week. Can I tell him you sent me?"

"Sure. It's called X-odus. On 7 Mile Road off I-94. I would dance there, too, but my dad won't let me."

"Good for him. I wouldn't let you either, if I were your dad!"

"Thanks, I think," Deanna laughed.

Deanna gave me her father's name and the address of the bar. Bill and I went there after work the next day. I did a little audition for him by walking into the bar, dancing and stripping as I moved toward him.

"You're hired!" he said.

"Cool. My name is Layne, and this is my husband, Bill. Deanna told me about your bar and that I might be able to get a part-time job here."

He laughed. "Now my daughter is finding dancers for me. Glad to meet you Layne and Bill." He extended his hand and shook ours. "My name's Jason, but everyone calls me Jay."

Bill said, "Glad to meet you. I hear this is a safe club."

"Yes," Jay said. "We have rules about touching and we have a bouncer, so we don't have trouble here very often. You should feel safe here."

So I stripped one night a week. Bill came to watch

me dance, and that kept him interested in me for a while. That bought me more time to work on my new plan for the future.

Irene was a rich bitch at the barn. She was my new plan. Irene treated everyone like servants, and no one liked that. I didn't like it either, but I could tolerate it. For a while.

11 - THE NEW PLAN

I always have a plan, and when Bonnie introduced me to Irene, I knew I had found what I needed. Irene was married to a rich and powerful man. And Irene didn't have any friends at the barn except Bonnie. I decided to be her friend.

But it wasn't easy. There was a lot of ass-kissing if you wanted to be Irene's friend. And I wanted to be her friend. So I got really good at ass-kissing.

Irene and I could form a partnership. Irene could finance the farm and have a built-in trainer and company in the form of boarders. Or she could just collect horses and show or breed them. I would get my farm and be guaranteed horses for life. It was perfect. Of course, I didn't tell her that.

There was just one problem: Bonnie. I had to make myself more valuable to Irene than Bonnie. Irene depended on Bonnie for everything at the farm because she didn't have any friends there. I didn't know why she didn't have any friends because she was beautiful and wealthy, but she was aloof and snotty to everyone, except the barn help. But the barn help weren't rich enough to be her friends, and I don't think she wanted them to be, either.

Irene spent all her time at the barn with Bonnie and

depended on her for lessons and the training of her horses. I had to ride better than, or at least as good as, Bonnie and be more available to Irene than Bonnie. She was my only rival for BFF with Irene because no one liked Irene, either.

Even Susan, Bonnie's mother, who liked everyone and was available to anyone, didn't really like Irene. She was courteous to her, but she didn't like her.

Eventually, Susan decided she didn't like me either. I overheard her tell Bonnie she shouldn't have hired me, and that she would probably be sorry she did in the long run. After hearing that, I was constantly looking for little ways to annoy Susan.

It was hard to get close to Irene. At first, I thought it would be easy, but I was wrong. Irene came to the barn almost every day and rode Parcel in a lesson or in a practice session. Then she watched Bonnie ride her young horse, Fortunate, who was in training with Bonnie. Other than that, Irene rode and was gone. She always handed her horse off to the barn help after her lesson or a practice ride. After that, she roared off in her Maserati before I could even start a conversation with her.

It wasn't until I had been at the barn for 3 months that I had a chance to talk to her. I was patient. I had been watching her and planning my attack for weeks, but didn't get a chance to get near her until I caught her watching Cyra ride one afternoon.

Irene was standing at the arena rail, watching Cyra

ride her horse, Chimmy, in a lesson with Bonnie. I knew Irene particularly hated Cyra, and I was confused to see her watching her ride.

I stepped up to the rail and stood by Irene. "She's a good rider," I said.

"Yes," Irene said, not taking her eyes off Cyra.

It was awkward. I had watched Irene ride her senior horse, Parcel, in a lesson the hour before, so I said, "Did you have a good lesson today?"

Irene turned and looked at me. I mean, her eyes scanned me from head to toe. I think I blushed. I almost turned around to leave.

"Not really," Irene said and tilted her nose up.

"Oh. Why not? Was Parcel naughty?"

"No," Irene sighed. "It's me. I just lose patience with him." Irene shifted her long legs and turned slightly away from me to watch Cyra.

Irene was being honest, and I had no idea how to respond to her. Fortunately, she continued talking. "I wish I could ride like Bonnie and Cyra or you, but I'm stiff and I forget to breathe."

"That's a problem we all either have, or have had," I said. "I'm sure it also took Bonnie a while to master being relaxed and totally in control of the horse's body as well, as her own."

"I hope you're right. I just got back into riding 2 years ago, after not riding since I was a kid."

"Really? Then I would say you're doing great!"

"Do you think so? Bonnie and everyone else here

make it look so effortless."

Wow. Irene was really opening up to me. I had hit the jackpot. I just needed to keep it going and not mess it up. I had an idea.

"I think you just need to ride more horses and maybe get a little tired. Sweat a little. Go on trail rides."

"Maybe you're right," Irene said, "but I don't want to ride Fortunate until I get better. I don't want to ruin him. He's so young. Bonnie's doing a great job with him, but I could wreck his confidence. And I don't want to take Parcel on trail rides. He's a show horse, and he's happy with that. I don't think Bonnie would approve, anyway."

Even though I bristled when Irene kept talking about Bonnie, I was happy that she was talking to me. I had to keep her talking.

"Maybe you need a horse to ride just for fun. One you can take on the trails. You could ride with me. I go out on the trails at least once a day. It's relaxing."

"Really? I would love to do that."

Jackpot. I took a deep breath. "Okay. I'll find you a horse to just have fun on, and we can ride together." Seal the deal, I was thinking.

"Sounds good." Irene tilted her head back and looked down at me. She was tall and beautiful. A cold, rich, beautiful bitch. Oh well, I could deal with it. Close the deal, I thought.

"I'll find you a horse that will make you a better rider for your other horses. I assume you'll be riding for the rest of your life?"

"Absolutely."

"Okay. I'll find you the perfect fun horse. Give me a few days. By the way, my name is Layne."

"Glad to meet you, Layne."

"Same here."

Finally, I was in. Now to find the sturdy, patient horse she needed, and work my magic.

It didn't take long. Summer was ending, and school would be starting up soon. A lot of kids were taking off for college and the parents who didn't own a farm were not always willing to pay board on a horse that was no longer being used. I had a lot of horses to choose from.

I chose a 12-year-old palomino gelding. He was tall and sturdy, with a calm temperament, and he was handsome. He had a flaxen mane and tail, a beautifully centered blaze connected to a snip on his soft muzzle, and 4 stockings. He would make Irene look good and tolerate her impatience. And the price was right.

I put $100 down on him and told Irene about him the next day.

"He's beautiful and kind, and the price is right," I told her.

"How much?"

"Nine thousand."

"Cash?"

"Yes."

Actually, the horse was priced at $7,000, but I figured

Irene would want me to trailer him to the barn, and I deserved a commission for finding him. But I didn't need to tell her all that.

"Okay. I'll bring the money tomorrow."

"I'll pick him up tomorrow afternoon," I told her.

True to her word, Irene handed me an envelope with nine thousand dollars in cash the next day. I removed two thousand dollars and put it in my wallet and picked up the horse that afternoon.

And so began my friendship plan with Irene.

12 - BESTIES

It wasn't long before Irene and I were best friends. Not only did we ride together every day, but we also went to lunch almost every day. Irene named him Oliver. She was still a stiff and impatient rider, but the palomino ignored her, and didn't hold a grudge.

As I said, Irene and I went to lunch almost daily and sometimes shopping too. Irene paid for everything. She had gotten so dependent on me that sometimes she texted me as soon as she drove into the barn parking lot. "I'm here," she would text.

"Do you want to ride or go to lunch first?" I would text back.

When she started looking for me the minute she entered the barn, I felt the time was right for the next step in my plan.

"Irene, what do you want more than anything in the world?" I asked her one day as we waited for our lunch and sipped cocktails.

Irene looked down at her drink and rubbed it with her finger. "A baby."

I was stunned. A baby? "A baby?" I said. "Why?"

"Because that's the best and only thing I can give Joey," she said, still looking at her drink.

"Oh." I didn't know what to say. I waited for her to

ask me what I wanted, but she didn't ask.

I had blown it.

Irene was in a down mood the rest of the day. Gone was the frozen ice-queen bitch. What was left was a morose shell of a person, going through the motions of being a dressage rider.

It was a relief when she tossed me Parcel's reins and said, "See you tomorrow."

I was putting Parcel in his stall when Bonnie walked by with Fortunate. "Irene was in a mood, wasn't she?" she said. "Usually, she stays to watch me ride Fortunate."

I shrugged. "She wants to have a baby."

"A baby?"

"That's what I said," I said and laughed.

"Oh, well. To each their own, I guess," Bonnie said.

I closed the stall door on Parcel and leaned on it. "You don't want children?"

Bonnie looked at me with a frown. "I'm almost forty. I never took an interest in men, and I was always too busy with this place, so now it's too late. Anyway, that's my excuse. How about you and Bill? Are you going to have children?"

I've always been outspoken, and Bonnie wouldn't use my honesty against me, so I just shrugged and said, "Bill wants them, but I don't even like sex!"

Bonnie laughed and hi-fived me, then walked on with Fortunate without saying another word.

It took a few days before Irene returned to her aloof

but Layne-dependent self. She didn't come to the barn for two days, but it was the weekend, and I figured she probably had plans with Joey. The horse shows were over for the year and Irene loved Joey "to the moon and back," as the teens in the barn were fond of saying.

Monday was my day off. I spent Mondays doing boring stuff like grocery shopping, cleaning house and laundry. Bill and I visited his parents every Monday night for dinner. Mondays were not fun.

But when Irene didn't come to the barn on Tuesday or Wednesday, I started to worry. I went through the morning, wondering what to do.

Finally, I called her cell phone.

When she answered cooly, "Yes?" I hesitated. What should I say?

"Irene, are you okay?"

"I'm okay. I just needed a break. I needed time to think about things. You know, about having a baby."

"Are you coming to the barn today?"

"I guess so. I should. Okay. I'll get dressed."

Damn. She was really down. "Get dressed and text me when you get here. I'm starving," I said.

Irene managed a little laugh. "You're always hungry," she said quietly.

"Not for food. I miss you, girl. Go get dressed!"

"K." Irene hung up.

We drank a whole bottle of wine before eating lunch, and Irene seemed to relax a little. I told her how I had stolen Susan's keys off her desk and left them in the restroom, causing her to waste the major part of the morning looking for them. Irene laughed and shook her finger at me.

Susan doesn't like Irene, and I think she likes me even less, so I was always looking for ways to annoy her. Irene thought that was funny, and, to tell the truth, I did too.

Then I told her about the new barn help and Bonnie's ride on Fortunate that morning.

"Almost all you ever talk about is horses and the barn," Irene said, smiling.

"That's because that's all I ever cared about. All my life," I said.

Irene just nodded.

I took a deep breath. Here goes, I thought. The next step in my plan.

"What I want more than anything," I said slowly, "is a barn of my own."

"Really?" Irene said, but didn't look at me or say anything more.

"Yes, all I need is a place of my own." I looked at Irene, but she had lost interest.

"I know you want a baby more than anything," I said. "I can see that now."

Irene looked at me. Her eyes were blank. "I've been trying to get pregnant for 5 years. I'm 27 now. I don't think it's gonna happen."

That was it. My cue. I could seal the deal if I worked

it right. "You need to forget about it. Then you'll get pregnant."

"What?"

"Yes," I said. "It happens all the time. Women give up and then they get pregnant! You've heard of all the couples who adopted, and then found out they were pregnant?"

"Sure. It happens all the time. But Joey is against adoption, and I want to give him his own flesh and blood. It's really important to him, and I want to give him that."

"So... here's the deal," I said. "Go into business with me. Board horses, breed horses, buy horses, train horses, sell horses. Get so busy, you won't have time to think about trying to get pregnant, and you'll get pregnant!"

Irene looked at me and grinned. "You're right! Let's do it!"

Wow. That was easy.

13 - PLANNUS INTERRUPTUS

But things didn't work out the way I wanted them to work out. Bill drank too much when we went to the club, and we got into an argument every time on the way home. He told me he no longer wanted to support my "horsey ambition," and I started thinking about killing him for his insurance money. But I would have to convince him to increase the amount of the policy first.

And things weren't moving very fast with Irene, either. I found a couple of farms online that looked pretty good but, when we saw them in person, they weren't as pretty as the pictures, and most of them needed a lot of updates or more land to give me what I wanted.

So I was getting a little frustrated at both jovs and at home. I had to find ways to lighten my load, so I started thinking of more ways to annoy Susan.

The first thing I did was buy a burner cell phone and assume the identity of a prospective boarder. I named her Julie.

Julie texted Susan and told her she owned 2 horses and would be moving to the area in a few months. Julie was interested in dressage lessons and also needed her young horse trained.

Susan responded with cheer, "Great! We can do that."

Then Julie proceeded to question Susan, a few questions at a time, each morning, about everything in the barn: barn hours, feeds and the amount fed, the type of hay and the amount fed, how many turnouts were available at the farm, and how many horses were turned out in each, who the farrier was, what vet clinic the farm used, how many boarders were at the farm, how many lessons were given a week, how much the farm charged for extra services such as blanketing and un-blanketing, etc., etc., etc.,...

Then Julie disappeared.

The next prank I pulled on Susan was to make online appointments for lessons with her or Bonnie, and then cancel them an hour or less before the lesson.

After a few canceled lessons, I looked around for other ways to annoy Susan, but, beyond the occasional opportunity to hide her keys or let the air out of her car's tires, I was finding it hard to come up with more ideas for pranks. I even put a rubber spider in her mailbox, but Susan, having been in a barn all her life, wasn't afraid of spiders.

Life was getting dull.

Eventually, Irene grew tired of Oliver and asked me to sell him. I think he was boring to her because he didn't give her any problems. Irene was a complicated person. Hard to figure out and hard to manipulate, but

I won this one.

"How about donating him to the farm as a lesson horse?" I asked her.

"Good idea," Irene said and walked away.

So I guess it was all up to me. I walked down the aisle and knocked on Susan's office door.

"Come in!" she sounded impatient.

I opened the door and walked in slowly. I knew Susan didn't like me, and I didn't like her back for that reason. Plus, I'm a little afraid of her, too. I walked in, but I stayed by the door and left it open a bit.

Susan put down the paper she had been reading and pulled off her reading glasses. She slowly laid them on top of the paper.

I cleared my throat. "Um, Irene wants to donate Oliver to your lesson program." I said.

Susan hesitated, then shook her head. I was ready to bolt out the door.

"Well, Layne, you continue to surprise me. I was just looking for another lesson horse." She patted the paper she had been reading. "Oliver is perfect. I accept, and please let Irene know she will get a tax write-off for the donation."

"I will, but I don't think she cares about a tax write-off."

"Very well," Susan said, and I thought I was being dismissed. I turned to go out the door. "And Layne?"

"Yes?" I turned halfway to look at Susan.

"Stop taking my keys and doing the other things."

I gulped and managed a nod, then left quickly. I heard Susan laughing after I closed the office door.

14 - EVERYONE'S FRIEND

I had been working at the farm for a little over a year when Marsha came to the barn with Real. I didn't know it then, but my life was about to change drastically.

It wasn't long before Marsha made friends with almost everyone at the barn. She was that kind of person: easy to get to know and easy to like.

She made friends with Cyra and Irene, two of the most unfriendly people in the barn. I didn't mind her getting friendly with Cyra. No one cared about Cyra But she was getting too friendly with Irene.

Don't get me wrong. Irene was still a bitch, and she was a bitch to Marsha. But Marsha persisted, as if she had a moral obligation to befriend everyone, including bitches. I didn't need Marsha getting in the way of my plans for Irene. I had to do something about Marsha. But what? I thought about it for a while... and came up with nothing.

Marsha was spared. For a while. In fact, everyone was spared for a while because I decided I would also become everyone's friend...

... *continued in Marsha's story:* **FALLING IN LOVE**

FALLING IN LOVE
Marsha's story

DEDICATION

This is dedicated to my late husband Joel. You opened the doors to all my dreams. I love you.

15 - AL

I brushed my horse and watched my husband flirt with Cyra. I was pretty sure Al was flirting, even though his words were innocent.

"How long have you been riding?" he asked her.

Cyra was squatting by her horse's legs, removing exercise boots. When she looked up to answer him, Al got what he was probably looking for: a magnificent view of Cyra's equally magnificent cleavage. I made a mental note to ask her, if I ever talked to her, how she kept her breasts from bouncing when she sat the trot.

"I've been riding all my life. I rode strapped to my mother's back when I was a baby and I sat in front of my sister when I was a toddler," Cyra told Al. "She gave me the reins and taught me the basics," she added as she stood up and unbuckled the girth on her saddle,

"And you're still taking lessons?" Al was genuinely surprised.

Cyra looked at Al. "I'll always take lessons. Even Olympic riders have coaches. I will probably need someone's eye on me for the rest of my riding life," she said, pulling the saddle off her horse's back. I saw the corner of Al's mouth twitch as he watched Cyra take her saddle into the tackroom.

I looked down at my brown riding breeches,

brown riding boots and the sleeve of my army green sweater. I hadn't bothered with make-up that morning and, at 5' 2", heavy in the hips, and small in the chest, I felt dumpy and plain compared to Cyra's curves and bright peacock colors.

Cyra was taller than me, and athletically built, with upright, round boobs. Today she was dressed in her usual bright colors and adorned with piercings on her nose, lips, tongue, ears and probably other places, too. Her black hair was streaked with purple and her eyes were blackened with makeup. Even her lips were black. To complete her colorful, sexy look, she wore a pink and purple tank top, purple full seat breeches and black riding boots with pink socks peeking out of the top of her boots.

Cyra went into the tackroom, and Al finally turned back to me. I dropped my eyes to my horse and brushed his spotlessly clean hide.

"I have to be out of town this weekend. A case came up suddenly, so I stopped in to let you know that I'm leaving. If this case can be settled quickly, I will be back on Monday."

I looked at my husband. Al was a foot taller than me, 37 years old and 13 years my senior. He was dressed in a dark blue business suit, a shade lighter blue tie, and an immaculate white shirt. His wavy black hair and choice of dark suit made his blue eyes sparkle. He looked smooth, professional and handsome. I felt my face blush when I looked at him.

"Okay," I said, but it felt as if someone just sucked all the energy out of my body. Another weekend away. Maybe it was time to talk to a private detective. Maybe a detective could tell me why my husband worked so much and on so many weekends.

Al wouldn't discuss his work with me. It wouldn't be right, he said. Some of his cases were reported in the newspapers, but, even then, he wouldn't talk about them. My husband is an attorney who defends people accused of murder, rape and other criminal acts. Again and again, I would tell myself, "I have a very good life. Better to not think about it. Maybe Al is right to keep it all to himself," but I didn't really believe it.

Al kissed me on the cheek. "I'll call you," he said and squeezed my shoulder, while looking at me with his beautiful blue eyes.

I held my breath. I loved looking at him, but his words sounded like something you might say to an acquaintance and the squeezing of my shoulder was something you might do to a friend. The kiss on the cheek hurt. It seemed to say, "good friend, but nothing more."

Maybe I was expecting too much but my marriage felt like a friendship, not a romance. Friends don't keep secrets from each other, I thought.

My husband was beginning to feel like a stranger.

Al and I married after a very brief courtship. It was a large, beautiful wedding, and I was happy. But, after the honeymoon, I spent many nights alone. Al started spending more and more time with clients, or worked late in his office away from home, or in his office at home. Al was constantly working. Distracted at home, he didn't really ignore me, but he was never fully with me. He always seemed deep in thought but didn't tell me about his thoughts. I felt alone even when he was home.

The romance was gone. My role as his wife had become like a job and my function was to maintain our home and his lifestyle. Al spent most of his evenings at the office or in meetings. There were many weekends, like the one coming up, when I was alone. I became lonely and bored. I needed something to fill the emptiness.

That's why I bought a horse.

One afternoon, after spending the day watching soap operas, I called my mother. "Hi, Mom. I hope I'm not calling at a bad time. I know you just got out of work. Can you talk?"

"Sure. What's wrong?"

I flinched. My mother knew me too well. I took a deep breath. "Mom, I hate to complain, and I don't want to sound like a silly woman, but I'm bored. Al works all the time and I can't cook or clean enough to fill the hours." I didn't want to tell her I was worried about other women in his life.

"Marsha," my mother said patiently, "you've

worked hard all your life, ever since it was legal for you to work. At fourteen you were mucking stalls every day after school, taking care of other people's horses. You practically ran the stable when you went to college. Why don't you relax and enjoy the money and time Al has provided for you?"

"But he works all the time, Mom. I'm bored!"

"Honey, I know you love Al and miss him, but he has a job to do. A very well-paying job. You need to think about what else you love. Focus on that for a minute. What do you love almost as much as Al?"

I stopped breathing. I love horses.

My love of horses began when I was six years old. My mother bought me a pony ride at Richmond Good Ole Days, and from that time on, I dreamed of horses, drew horses and read about horses.

For my 12th birthday my mother took me to a local riding stable for my first riding lesson. I was hooked. I took weekly lessons until I turned fourteen and got a job at the stable. I turned out horses, cleaned their stalls, brought them back in and fed them in exchange for the use of a horse and riding lessons. Thanks to my work at Greenstone, I learned the "lower levels" of dressage and to jump, although jumping scared me a little. I continued to work at Greenstone when I went to Oakland University and got my associate's degree and a paralegal certificate.

After college and an internship at the Oakland

County Circuit Courthouse, I applied for a job at a private law firm in Grosse Pointe. I got the job and met Al. Thar's when my world changed.

Alton Myers was a partner at the firm, and he was very attentive to me from the first day I worked there. I thought the constant attention he gave me was simply to help me learn the job. I was embarrassed, flattered and a little nervous around him, and I thought that was due to my newness at the job.

But when he asked me to go to dinner and took me to New York in his private airplane, a Cessna Citation, I understood it was something more. That made me even more nervous.

I had never ridden in an airplane before, and I couldn't stop looking at the clouds.

"Better than horseback riding?" Al teased.

"No, but just as exciting," I replied with a nervous smile.

We landed at Teterboro Airport and parked the Cessna there. Al hired a chauffeur driven limousine for the short drive to New York City and then on to The View Restaurant & Lounge on the 48th floor of the Marriott. He ordered cocktails, and we watched Times Square and the streets of New York as the restaurant revolved. Al ordered wine with dinner and brandy after dinner.

"Are you trying to get me drunk?" I giggled. "Because, if you are, you succeeded. I'm revolving like the restaurant!" I covered my mouth and laughed.

Al shook his head and confessed, "Actually, the drinks were for me, so I could tell you..." Al sighed and raised both hands, as if giving up, "Marsha, I can't stop thinking about you! I have become obsessed with you. I think we should get married."

My mouth fell open. I dropped my head and tried to swallow. My heart was thumping, and it was hard to breathe. I put my hands on the table, trying to calm myself.

Al didn't seem to notice my nervousness. He reached over the table and covered my hands with his. "Let's go pick out a ring," he said quietly.

I looked at Al's hands. They felt good on mine, but I was scared. Who was this man? What was he talking about? Did I even hear him right? Finally, still looking at his hands, I said, "This is our first date. You don't know me. I don't know you."

"We will have more dates, but I already know a lot about you. I looked at your file." Al took his hands off mine. Then he touched my chin and lifted it, forcing me to look at him.

I thought he might be joking. But was he joking about knowing me or getting a ring? It might be both, so I smiled and tried to relax, "Anyway, it's 10 o'clock at night."

Al looked deep into my eyes and didn't smile. "It's New York, and something is always open. Look, this isn't rational, and it has nothing to do with common sense. I loved you from the moment I saw you. I've heard the saying 'love at first sight' and now I finally understand it." He took my hands in his. "Marry me," he said.

I stopped breathing and hoped Al didn't hear my heart thumping or feel the sweat gathering in my hand.

Three months later, we were married. It was easy to fall in love with Al. He did everything right. He was my Prince Charming, my knight in shining armor. I loved to be with him and would often lay awake at night to watch him sleep. I wondered how I had been lucky enough to marry such a man.

Our marriage gave me time and money, and that was something new in my life. Al didn't want me to work. He told me to spend my days doing whatever I wanted to do.

I tried to be the wife I thought Al wanted. I cleaned and decorated the house we bought in Grosse Pointe. I learned to cook and bake and made interesting, multi-course dinners, but Al didn't seem to care about my new skills. He usually worked from early morning into the night, and later, he started working on weekends.

I stopped cooking evening meals for him after a long series of cold dinners. The last dinner I cooked was a fresh garden salad with barbecue baby back ribs, seasoned potatoes and early asparagus. It sat on the table, untouched, until Al walked in the door at 10 pm.

I was sitting at the little breakfast table in our kitchen, staring at the unlit candle and the cold dinner that took an hour and a half to prepare.

"Hi," he said and kissed the top of my head.

"Dinner is ready," I said, without turning to face him.

"I'm not hungry." Al opened the refrigerator and grabbed a bottled water. "I ate in the conference room."

I got up and gathered our beautiful bone china plates with our untouched dinner on them and threw them in the waste bin under the kitchen sink. I closed the cabinet door and placed my hands on the rim of the sink. I was shaking, but I didn't know if I was going to explode in anger or cry.

Al put the bottle of water down, grabbed me by the shoulders, and turned me around to face him. Then I started crying.

My eyes were closed, and I couldn't open them. Al took me in his arms and held me until my shoulders relaxed and I put my arms around him. After a few minutes, he turned my face to his and wiped away my tears.

I opened my eyes, but couldn't look at Al. I looked at his shirt.

"Marsha," he said slowly, "I can't always be home for dinners at night. I'm sorry I hurt you. I've been thoughtless, not calling when I'm tied up with clients or working. I've been a single man all my life. I've always lived this way. But I need to start thinking about how you feel. I'm sorry."

I nodded at Al's shirt.

"From now on, if I can make it home for dinner, I will call you and we can cook something together when I get home, or we can go out, or I can bring a take-out home for us. Okay?"

I nodded again and buried my face in his chest. Al picked me up and carried me to the bedroom. After making love, he retrieved the unbroken dishes from the waste bin, and put them in the dishwasher. Then he drew a bath for us, lit some candles and carried me to the bath. For one night, the romance was back.

Al continued to work late or out of town, and my dinners were usually eaten alone. Our beautifully equipped kitchen stayed immaculately clean and mostly unused.

I was bored. I bought house plants and watered them too much. I cleaned my beautiful house and watched too much daytime television. I slept too much. I gained weight. I began to paint my nails and one day realized I had 41 bottles of nail polish.

I complained about it to my mother during one of our weekly visits. "Is this what my life will be? I've been collecting bottles of nail polish! Nail polish! I spent this morning counting bottles and making a chart of the colors and painted little squares on the chart for each color!"

My mother laughed. "Why are you so silly? You

can do anything you want, you lucky girl. I shouldn't have to ask you again, but I will. What, besides Al, is important to you?"

I stopped breathing. Horses.

"I can hear it in your silence," my mother laughed again. "Like I told you last week, go get yourself a horse. It's okay. You can afford one now."

I laughed. "You're right. Yes, I can." I hugged my mom and laughed again. "It's just hard to believe that now I can really afford a horse. I guess I'll just have to do it and then I'll believe it."

A horse of my own. I could finally afford one, and I certainly had enough time for riding. I took a deep breath and started to feel alive again.

16 - REAL

I knew exactly what kind of horse I wanted. I wanted a dressage horse who could climb the "levels" with me, but who would tolerate the mistakes I would make along the way. And I wanted a young horse with a clean vet check since "school masters," older trained horses that had "been there, done that," were hard to find, expensive and usually had soundness issues.

At the end of two months, I looked at and rode 17 horses, but found nothing suitable. I looked online, called, emailed, looked at videos, traveled to see and ride horses, and got the few who seemed suitable vet checked. All my efforts had led to frustration and disappointment. It was emotionally exhausting, and I almost wanted to give up, but the thought of not having a horse, now that I could actually afford one, made me keep looking.

My search continued into the third month and I wasn't hopeful when I saw an ad for a "real gentleman training at 4th Level." All the horses I had previously looked at had catchy phrases in their ads like "perfect amateur's horse" or "ready to show" but all had fallen short on attitude, training or soundness.

This ad referred to a bay gelding with matching hind socks and an irregular star. He was a Dutch

Warmblood gelding with excellent breeding, 9 years old, and being sold because his owner was moving to South Africa. The conformation photos showed that the gelding had a short back and long, correct legs. The ad described him as 16 hands, with smooth gaits, shown 3rd Level and training at 4th. He was stabled only 60 miles away in a village called Holly, so I made an appointment to see him, although I expected to be disappointed again.

I arrived at the barn a few minutes late. The trainer was waiting for me, leaning against the barn door. He greeted me without a smile, but said nothing about my tardiness. He just nodded and said, "Are you here to see Lad?"

I nodded in reply.

The trainer said, "Follow me."

I slipped my helmet bag over my shoulder and followed him. I was a bit surprised at my rudeness, but I was feeling grumpy and thinking I was probably wasting my time, anyway.

We walked in silence down a dimly lit corridor. I could see the barn's indoor arena through a couple of open doorways in the corridor. The corridor connected to a small stable area at the end of the arena.

It took a minute for my eyes to adjust to the brighter light in the stable. The trainer walked to a stall where a bay gelding with a large irregular star was waiting, his head hanging over the half-door. I felt a tingle run down my spine, although I couldn't say why.

When the trainer brought the gelding out of his stall, "Lad" almost walked over him, right up to me, and put his head on my chest. As he pressed against me, I felt my grumpiness disappear. Finally, I took hold of his halter and stepped back to look at him. The gelding looked at me with large, clear eyes and I smiled.

The trainer took Lad from me, put him on cross-ties and saddled him. Lad stood quietly while the saddle was girthed, calmly watching me. The tightening of the girth did not irritate him, and that was a good sign. It meant that he wasn't saddle-sore and probably didn't have ulcers.

Then the trainer bridled him in a simple snaffle bridle. The bridle's noseband had an attachment for a flash strap, but the trainer didn't use one. That was another good sign. It meant that Lad did not open his mouth to avoid the action of the bit while being ridden.

The trainer led us to the indoor arena through a gate from the small barn. I expected him to lunge Lad, but he said, "Did you bring a helmet?"

I nodded and pulled my helmet from its bag and showed it to him.

"Put it on," he said.

I put my helmet on and snapped the chin strap. The trainer handed me the reins without comment.

I was surprised. When I looked at all the other sale horses, the trainers lunged them and rode them first, while making a sales pitch. This trainer apparently wasn't going to ride and said nothing about the horse. He just walked away and stood in the corner of the arena.

I walked Lad to the mounting block in the opposite corner of the arena. When I placed him beside it, he stood quietly with his neck slightly bent, watching me.

I adjusted the stirrups to a suitable length for my legs and climbed aboard. When I settled into the saddle, my legs fit comfortably along Lad's sides. I touched him with my calves, and he walked off calmly.

I pointed Lad to one of the dark openings in the arena wall. I counter-bent his neck slightly so he would have to focus on the dark area as we passed it. When he didn't spook as we passed, even when someone dropped something in the corridor, I smiled.

Then I trotted Lad across the arena, toward the doorway to the small barn. I wanted to see if he would try to duck out of the arena and go back to his stall. The tempo of Lad's trot never faltered as we moved past the entrance and rounded the corner on the short end of the arena.

As I rode Lad, I watched his ears swiveling back and forth, telling me that he was trying to understand what I wanted him to do. I smiled and did not think about anything but the horse moving under me. When the ride was over, I reluctantly handed the reins to the trainer. He didn't say anything and started walking back to the little barn entrance with Lad.

"I'd like to put a deposit on him and schedule a vet

check," I said to the trainer's back.

He nodded.

"And thank you," I added.

The trainer stopped and turned around. "You're welcome," he said with another nod and a smile.

Lad passed the vet check, and I purchased him, but I had to leave him with the trainer for a few days while I searched for a dressage-oriented barn within a reasonable driving distance from my home.

At 9 o'clock on the morning after Lad's successful vet check, I sat at the kitchen table with my cell phone fully charged and my laptop open. I put my hand on Lad's registration papers, which the trainer handed to me on the day Lad passed the vet check and I purchased him. "My horse," I whispered and smiled.

Lad's registered name was Latimer's Gold, and he was called Lad, but I decided to give him a new barn name. "Real" was more dignified, I thought, and the perfect name for my dream horse, who had become real.

Looking online, I found several stables in the 45 mile radius I was willing to travel, but only one dressage barn. The other barns were western-oriented, hunter-jumper or lesson barns, like the barn of my teenage years. The only dressage barn located at a suitable distance from Grosse Pointe was Centerline Farm, located in Muttonville, a part of Richmond, and not far from my mother's apartment in the same town. That gave me another thing to smile about.

A woman who identified herself as Susan answered the phone when I called Centerline Farm.

"Hi Susan," I said. "My name is Marsha. I just purchased a dressage horse. He passed his vet check, he has health papers and a Coggins and he needs a new home. He's beautiful and kind," I added, out of breath and feeling like a proud parent.

"Good for you!" Susan replied. "What's his level and what are your goals?"

I gave Susan a brief summary of my riding skills and added, "I'd like to take lessons and compete in dressage. Real is trained to Third Level and schooling Fourth, but, as I said, I've only ridden to Second Level."

"Well, it sounds like you chose the right horse. When would you like to visit the farm and interview?"

"Now? Sorry. I mean, whenever you're available. I don't want to sound too eager, but I'm anxious to get Real moved and start riding again."

"Of course. I understand! Well, let's see..." I could hear pages turning, probably in a book or calendar. "I am available anytime today, but I want you to meet Bonnie, my daughter, and our assistant trainer, Layne. Bonnie is free at 2 this afternoon. If you can be here around 1, I can give you a tour first."

"Great," I said. "I'll be there at 1 o'clock."

"See you then," Susan said.

I put the phone down and smiled. I felt alive again.

17 - CENTERLINE FARM

The entrance to Centerline Farm was framed by a cobblestone fence. A cast iron logo of a prancing horse and the legend "Centerline Farm" was mounted on the right side of the coblestone fence.

Paddocks lined each side of the driveway and the horses in them were quietly grazing and swatting their tails at spring flies. It seemed idyllic. I could see four horses on my left and three on my right as I drove slowly down the driveway, gravel crunching under my car's tires.

The barn was about 500 feet beyond the entrance. As I drove closer, I raised an eyebrow. The barn had a rectangular face and a second floor with curtained windows. A roofed patio area lined the front of the barn and held chairs and benches made from tree limbs and slabs of wood. Hanging baskets of pansies and flower boxes bursting with tulips separated the patio area from the parking lot.

The parking lot extended to the left side of the building where two large trailers connected to semi-trucks and a detached gooseneck trailer with living quarters sat, with the "Centerline Farm" logo on their sides. Smaller horse trailers were parked beside them. On the right side of the barn there was a driveway.

Probably for deliveries, I thought.

I parked in front of the barn where other cars and trucks sat behind a barrier fence. Then I headed for a door in the center of the building.

Inside the building, I paused a moment. Susan had told me to turn left, and I would find the office at the end of the aisle.

I turned left and walked slowly. The stalls were on my left. All had half-doors, allowing the horses to hang their heads out. One horse stopped eating hay and stared at me.

"Hi, big guy," I said.

The horse blew softly at me, then dropped his head and continued to eat.

Every stall seemed to be occupied even the ones that didn't have horses in them. There were droppings in the empty stalls and horses munching hay in all the others. I wondered if they had a stall for Real, and if they didn't, how long Real would have to wait for one, if they accepted me as a boarder.

At the end of the aisle, I saw a door marked "Office" and headed toward it. When I was a few feet away from the door, it flew open and I jumped a little.

A short, muscular woman with greying blonde hair came out and laughed. "I'm sorry. I didn't mean to scare you. You must be Marsha?"

I exhaled and smiled. "Hi. And you must be Susan?"

"Yes, glad to meet you, Marsha. I'll show you the barn and then you can meet Bonnie. She's giving a lesson right now. She's my daughter. I think I told you?"

I nodded yes, afraid to interrupt the little ball of energy in front of me. As she talked, Susan walked, and motioned me to follow her down the aisle.

"Layne is our assistant trainer and she teaches riders up to FEI Level. Layne's from South Dakota. Right now, she's riding one of our young horses in training. You'll meet her soon. And we have several working students. You can meet them and some of the boarders later."

I almost bumped into Susan when she stopped suddenly. "This is the tackroom for this aisle." Susan opened a door in the wall across from the row of stalls I had just passed. The aroma of fine leather floated toward me. She flipped on a light and I saw a line of dressage saddles and bridles mounted on the wall. A row of identical trunks rested beneath the saddles.

"Very nice," I said, smiling.

"We have tackrooms on both aisles. There are twelve stalls on this aisle and twenty on the back side of the arena. There is a small barn, also attached to the arena, for our broodmares. lesson horses and ponies. I can show you all that later, or on another day, but let me show you the observation room now. Come this way."

I obediently followed, thinking, I like her. Susan reminded me of my mother. I followed her to the end of the aisle and up a flight of heavy wooden stairs to the observation room. "There is another set of stairs at the other end of the aisle," Susan said as we entered the room.

The observation room was large, spanning the entire front of the barn, and was about thirty feet in depth. The inner wall was made of large windows, allowing a full view of the indoor arena.

Several dark wood tables and chairs filled the center of the room. Susan pointed to a refreshment bar on the left. "There is a small kitchen behind it," she said. "You are welcome to use it to warm-up food if you bring a lunch. We have informal dinners here once in a while for the boarders."

The observation room felt spacious, welcoming and comfortable. I sighed, thinking it was the perfect place to watch riders or to relax and discuss things. I walked to the windows and looked down into the arena. Susan followed me.

A slender blonde woman was gesturing to a rider who circled around her.

"That's my daughter, Bonnie," Susan said. "The lesson will be over in a few minutes, and you can meet her then."

I turned and smiled at Susan, then noticed a group of framed photographs hanging on the wall to my left. Some photographs looked recent, but many of them were obviously old.

Susan turned to the wall. "That," she said, "is a photographic history of the farm."

I walked to the wall, and Susan followed. She pointed to a large photograph in the middle of the wall. "This is an aerial photo of Centerline Farm. We have sixty acres of land, and we grow most of our hay. There is a stream running through the back of the property and beyond that is land owned by the state." She traced a curved line under the glass of the photograph, indicating the stream. It was a small stream, curving as it flowed southward.

"About 300 feet beyond the stream is state land. You can see the access road here." Susan pointed to the top of the map. "Our boarders often ride there, but trail riding can be unpredictable. A good trail horse has to be better trained than most, or at least even-tempered, because there are always surprises on the trail. A loose dog, a surprised deer or even a kid riding a bicycle can spook a horse. I ask everyone who rides the trails to ride in pairs or groups and wear helmets, but many of them don't."

Helmets were required for minors riding horses in Michigan, but the state law allowed adults to choose to wear one or not.

"I've always worn a helmet when riding, and I can't imagine riding without one," I said.

"Good." Susan nodded and continued, "In 1855 my great grandfather, Innis Casey, established a dairy farm here. The area was growing, and he knew it would need the meat and dairy products he could provide. He came from a dairy farming family, and they had built a successful business in New York. He was ready to strike out on his own and liked this area with access to the lakes and Canada. So he bought 120 acres and cut down trees. He used the trees for fences and buildings," she pointed to some structures in a photograph next to the aerial map, "and furniture."

I opened my mouth to ask a question, but Susan smiled and nodded. "Yes, the chairs amd tables on the front of the barn and in the observation room were designed after the furniture he made. We have a few original pieces in the house."

Susan looked at me. "Am I boring you?"

"Absolutely not," I shook my head and smiled. "Please continue?"

Susan smiled. "Then he brought stock from his family's farm in New York and set up his own dairy. After the Grand Trunk Railway came to this area in 1859, he made a lot of money by shipping his cheese, butter, and meat products to Union soldiers during the Civil War."

Susan pointed to a photograph of a man, a woman and five children. "This is him: my great grandfather Innis Casey. He was a very successful man. But he was busy. He married late in life. He married a local girl. She was sixteen, and he was sixty. He fathered four sons. One was my grandfather, and his fifth child was a daughter, my greataunt Eleanor. Everyone called her Nellie or Aunt Nellie."

Susan paused and looked at me. "Still not bored?"

"No," I answered truthfully. "This is fascinating."

Susan nodded and continued, "After his death, the farm was divided, according to his will, between the sons, leaving thirty acres to each son. But Nellie was not included in the division of the land. Maybe her father thought she would marry and didn't need land, but Nellie never married. She was a schoolteacher and lived with one of the brothers, Grady, a bachelor. When Grady died at a young age, she inherited his portion of the farm."

Susan smiled. "After her Grady's death, Nellie and her brothers kept the dairy farm going, even though the property had been divided." She pointed to a faded photograph of a smiling woman in overalls with one leg braced on the running board of a shiny black Ford Model T. I understood that this was Aunt Nellie.

"The overalls were a scandal at that time!" Susan laughed. "Aunt Nellie smoked cigarettes and, when she was at home, dressed like a man. Some of the locals were disturbed by her male demeanor and wanted to get her fired as a teacher, but it never happened. She was an excellent teacher, and I think she had a little dirt on the right people!" Susan winked at me and looked back at the photograph.

"I took that photo with the Brownie camera she gave me for my 16th birthday. I still have the camera. Aunt Nellie's the reason Centerline Farm exists."

"Really? Wow, what a history! Thank you for sharing that with me," I said.

"My pleasure." Susan looked at her watch. "Let's go see Bonnie. Her lesson should be over by now."

The next half hour was spent with Bonnie, who had light brown hair that was streaked blonde by the sun and pulled back into a ponytail. She was tall and slender with small breasts and hips, and had a lean, tanned physique. She wore no makeup but was a natural beauty with golden brown eyes framed by brown eyelashes and perfectly shaped eyebrows.

When Susan introduced me to Bonnie, she smiled and reached out to shake my hand. I took her hand, and she pumped mine once and said, "Hi."

I met the assistant trainer, Layne, at the same time. She was walking her training horse down the aisle and Susan stopped her. "Layne, this is Marsha. She's viewing the barn today."

Layne responded by introducing me to the horse she was leading. "Hi, Marsha. This is Victor. He's a 3-year-old Westphailian, owned by Janet Hoskins." She gave the youngster a noisy pat. Victor shook his head and put his ears back. Layne frowned at him.

I offered my hand to Victor. He put his ears forward, sniffed at my hand and rubbed it with his muzzle, making me laugh.

"He likes you," Susan said.

"That's big," Layne said. "Victor doesn't like most people."

Layne was also tall and slim. Her auburn hair was

straight and thick, cut to a slight angle from the neck. It fell forward when she moved and touched her chin. Her thick hair partly covered her eyes, which were green and seemed to lighten or darken from minute to minute. Her eyebrows were thin and arched, her nose small, a little flared at the nostrils and her mouth was petite and pouty with a perfect "cupid's bow". She had a short chin and a flawless ivory complexion. Her face reminded me of a doll's face.

"Layne apprenticed under Craig Heckert, owner of Rivervale Farm in South Dakota," Bonnie told me. "Craig is one of only a few accomplished dressage trainers who teaches and trains in an isolated area."

That confused me. "Accomplished?"

Layne explained, "Yes, Craig has his gold medal. He worked hard and climbed the ladder to reach the top. It's not easy. Or cheap."

"Oh. Well, I guess I'm only on the second rung of the ladder," I said and felt my face get warm.

Bonnie smiled and nodded. "We can help," she said, then smiled as three young people entered the aisle, equipped with pitchforks and wheelbarrows.

"Hey guys, come meet Marsha," Susan waved them over. "Marsha owns a young Dutch Warmblood, and she is touring the barn. Marsha, meet our working students: Meghan, Carrie and Mitch."

Meghan was brown-haired and freckled She stepped forward with a smile and offered her hand to me. I shook it gratefully. Carrie and Mitch, both blonde, nodded and smiled at me, but didn't offer a handshake. I remembered my days as a working student and understood their shyness.

"We're proud of our working students," Susan told me and smiled at the three embarrassed young people. "They are an important part of our business and sometimes the only human a horse might interact with on a particular day if the owner doesn't come to the barn, or a trainer doesn't work with them."

I nodded, remembering the horses I had cared for as a teenager.

Susan interrupted my thoughts. "I'm going to leave you with Bonnie. I have to call in a feed order, but you can find me in the office when you're finished here."

I nodded at Susan's back because she had already turned and hurried down the aisle to her office. I felt a little dizzy and slow compared to Susan's energy.

Bonnie touched my elbow and said, "She's always busy. She doesn't stop until she falls asleep, and I think she would skip sleep if she could!"

I smiled and said, "That's my mother, too."

"My sympathies!" Bonnie laughed. "It's hard to keep up with mothers like that. Are you ready to meet two of our boarders?"

"Sure."

"Follow me," Bonnie said and took me to the end of the aisle where two young men were tacking up their horses. I was surprised to see that they were identical twins, and they were consciously or unconsciously mirroring each other, their horses face to face on the crossties in the barn aisle. The horses were chestnut geldings marked alike with four white socks and a wide ribbon of white down their broad faces.

Bonnie introduced me to them. "Hi, guys, this is Marsha. Marsha, meet Ben and Martin."

Both young men gave me a full-toothed, dazzling smile. "Hi, Marsha!" they said in unison.

I grinned at the twin's Cheshire cat faces. "Twins!" I said and immediately thought that was a stupid thing to say. Of course, they were twins. "Ben and Martin?" I said and winced. Now I sounded like a parrot.

"Yes," Ben said. "Our Mom wanted to be able to tell us apart!" He raised his eyebrows and laughed.

It took me a second, then I laughed too. "Like that would help!"

"Sorry," Martin said. "Ben thinks he's funny."

Ben punched Martin on the arm. "You always say it first! I beat you to it this time."

"Touché," Martin said. "Actually, he came first," he jerked his thumb toward Ben, "so he was named for our father. I was last so I was named for our mother."

I frowned. "For your mother? Martin?"

"Yeah. Our mother drank too many martinis and got pregnant!" He and Ben burst out laughing.

"Sorry," Ben said. "I apologize for my younger brother's behavior. He was named for our mother's father."

"Oh," I said. I was getting uncomfortable being the

straightman for their jokes, so I tried to change the subject, "What are your horse's names?"

"This is Caesar," Ben said.

"And this is Julius!" Martin told me.

I shook my head and laughed.

Then Ben said "Hey, Marsha, do you have a photo of your horse? Where did he come from? What's your horse's name? What level do you ride?"

Martin chimed in: "What shows are you going to this year? Are you going to Florida with us? Where did you train before? What kind of scores did you get? Are you tired yet?" and both of them laughed.

"Very funny, guys," Bonnie said. "Give her a break! Sorry, Marsha. They think they're a tag team. They do this kind of thing to everyone new."

"Seriously, welcome to the barn!" Ben and Martin said together.

"Thank you," I said, and wished I had something funny to add.

Bonnie rescued me from the twins and gave me a quick tour of the rest of the building. "There are 30 horses boarded at Centerline, including horses in training," she said as we walked down the back aisle, behind the arena. We have three broodmares in the barn in back, as well as lesson horses and ponies." She pointed to a barn attached to the end of the arena. You can see them later. Right now, they are in the back pasture."

I didn't get to see all the boarder's horses either, but

the horses that were inside seemed friendly. Waiting for training, lessons or their turnout, they leaned over their half-doors and sniffed my hand. Their eyes were large and happy, clearly healthy and secure with their place in life. This is the right place for Real, I thought. He would love it here.

Bonnie looked at her watch. "I have a lesson in five minutes with the twins. You are welcome to watch, or you can find my mother in the office. Thank you for visiting Centerline," she said, and she extended her hand to me.

I took Bonnie's hand, received a firm grip, and then she was gone.

I found my way back through the barn aisles to Susan's office. The door was cracked open, but I knocked, anyway.

"It's Marsha," I said through the opening.

"Come in!" Susan called out.

I pushed open the door to see Susan standing at her desk. "Come in," she said and waved me inside. "Please sit down," she said, turning her wave to the chair in front of her desk.

I obediently sat and waited. Behind Susan was a large photograph of the woman I recognized as Aunt Nellie, but in this photograph she had her hair up and she was dressed in a beautiful evening gown. Her left hand was draped over the neck of a large dog who looked as regal as she looked. A slightly smaller photo hung to the left of it: a muscular grinning man holding the reins of a spotted pony with a tiny blonde-haired girl sitting on it. On the right were three small photos of a skinny blonde girl in various stages of her life with horses. Bonnie, of course.

"Where are the photos of you?" I asked.

Susan pointed to my right. I turned in my chair and saw that the wall to the right of her filling cabinet was covered with photos of Susan at various stages of her own life with horses.

Then I looked at the wall on the other side of the room. It held another large group of pictures: photos of Bonnie with horses. I turned around in my chair and saw that along both sides of the office door hung several elegant ribbons. Some were printed in English. Some were printed in foreign languages.

I turned around and smiled at Susan. "Do you have time to tell me about these photos?"

Susan laughed. "I'd be delighted to. It's basically the story of my life!" She indicated the photo behind the desk. "This is Aunt Nellie, of course. She was dressed for her 'coming out' party. It's the only formal picture we have of Aunt Nellie. I think her father was hoping to find a husband for her, but it didn't happen!

"I loved, and still love Aunt Nellie. Like I said, she is the reason Centerline Farm exits. I was crazy about horses when I was young and, of course, I wanted one, but my father said, You can't eat them! He was joking, but I didn't get a horse, either."

"But you had the land," I sympathized.

"No one in my family cared about horses. Not even Aunt Nellie. She preferred tractors. But she cared about me, and she supported me. She took me to a hunter-jumper barn for lessons. She paid for all my lessons and came to my shows. She even leased horses for me. Naturally, I wanted my own horse, but the barn owner told Aunt Nellie that leasing was better than owning, and that I could lease different horses and learn more that way. Aunt Nellie agreed and I always had a leased horse. She paid for everything. I guess I was her surrogate child because she never married and didn't have children. She was always there for me."

Susan sighed. "My parents didn't want any part of it. Even after I won championships on the leased horses, my parents and my brother and sister didn't care, but Aunt Nellie stood by me." Susan laughed and shook her head. "No one argued with Aunt Nellie!"

"I was eventually offered a job at a barn and paid for my own lessons," Susan continued. "I worked at Sugarbush Farm in Chesterfield. Maybe you've heard of it? It's gone now, but it was the place to be when I was young. Aunt Nellie bought me a truck when I told her about the job so I could drive myself to work. I told her a car would have been cheaper. Do you know what she said?" Susan asked.

"I have no idea."

"She said, 'You're going to need a truck to haul horses to shows.' She thought of everything. Anyway,

Aunt Nellie was proud of me. She would drop by the barn occasionally and watch me work, cleaning stalls, turning out horses and tacking up school horses. Sometimes I would be riding a new horse that had just come to the barn. She would watch and never say a word. The horse might buck or rear or try to brush me off on a fence. I worked through the problem and got the horse comfortable, but she never commented on it. Just watched and left. I never knew when or if she would show up."

Susan's face saddened, but she continued her story. "I never knew what she thought of my ambitions until she died. After I graduated from high school, I didn't go to college. My father was very angry, and when I used all the money I had saved to buy my first horse, he wouldn't speak to me."

Susan pointed to a faded photograph of a thin, dull-coated gelding. "I took this picture of Rumor when I was thinking about buying him and he was still at the racetrack. He was thin and kind of ugly. He was just a plain bay gelding and too lazy to race, but that helped him stay sound until I found him. I bought him dirt cheap. Turned out, he could jump the moon!" Susan laughed.

"Rumor gave me his trust and years of ribbons. He was retired, still sound, and enjoyed lazy school horse days as my 'babysitter' schoolmaster. He taught dozens of children to ride," Susan said. "This is the last photo I have of him." Susan pointed to a large framed photo.

I stood and looked closely at the picture of Rumor. He had become beautiful under Susan's care. His muscles bulged beneath a gleaming coat and his black mane and tail were thick and waving in the wind. He was looking into the distance, and he seemed to be thinking, "Life is good!"

"After I bought Rumor, I started my lesson and training business. I would travel from barn to barn, giving lessons or training horses for people." Susan pointed to photos of herself surrounded by trophies and ribbons. "I showed horses for people, got a few 'catch rides' at shows and bought and sold horses. I knew that, someday, I would have my own farm."

Susan cleared her throat. "My father died when he was only fifty years old, and I bought my father's part of the original Casey farm from my mother. No one could believe that I got a bank loan to buy the farm. Banks weren't giving loans to self-employed single women at that time, but I got the loan," Susan said and smiled. "It was probably because Aunt Nellie and the owner of Sugarbush pushed it through the bank for me!"

Susan joined me at the wall. She pointed to another photo. "This is an old photo of Aunt Nellie's part of the farm. Remember, I told you she inherited it from Uncle Grady, her bachelor brother?"

I nodded.

"Well, as I said, I didn't know what Aunt Nellie thought of my decision to make horses my career until she died. Aunt Nellie died three years after my father.

She left her portion of the original dairy farm, which she inherited from her brother, to me. My brother and sister received some money from Aunt Nellie, but no land. Their money is gone now, but the land is still here." Susan nodded and pointed to an old aerial photo. "The back of Centerline Farm was her portion of the original dairy farm, next to this front part, which was my father's property." Susan pointed to another spot in the photo. "That building, an old dairy barn, is located to the east of the building we are standing in. It was my first horse barn. I took out the cattle stanchions and put stalls in. But now we use it for hay storage."

Susan folded her arms and looked at the photo. "I boarded horses, taught lessons, broke out young horses and did anything equine to maintain and improve the farm. When I got married, my husband, Max, became my biggest supporter." She pointed to a photograph of a muscular man, grinning at the camera as he tossed a bale of hay onto a wagon. I watched Susan's face change from pride to sadness as she looked at the photograph of her husband.

Then she turned away from the wall and looked at her watch. "Well, we can save the rest of the story for another day. Let's get the boarding contract filled out and make arrangements to get your horse here, okay?" Susan went back to her desk and took some papers from a drawer.

I nodded and wondered why I felt empty and sad. After all, I didn't know Max, and I had just met Susan.

I shivered a little and shook my self mentally.

I sat down in front of the desk and realized that Susan had a place for Real, and he would be boarding at Centerline. I smiled, then a question entered my mind. "Susan, do you have a screening process for accepting new boarders? I got the impression on the phone that you would interview me, but it seems the minute I walked in, I was accepted. I'm grateful for that, but I thought you screened potential boarders?"

"Absolutely!" Susan smiled. "I certainly do, and you passed with flying colors, so to speak."

I frowned, then smiled. "Oh, so how do you screen? Do you perform a background check before a potential boarder arrives, or did I miss something?" I laughed and said, "I'm sorry. I'm just curious."

"No, I don't do a background check or anything like that," Susan chuckled. She put her hands on the desk and clasped them together. "When you've been around horses as long as I have, you learn a few things. Horses can't talk. They pay attention to each other's body language. I learned to watch horses as they watch people. I watch their reactions to people."

Susan looked at me. "The impression I got from Victor and the others we passed today was a good one. They accepted you completely. That's all the screening I need." She smiled and pushed some papers across the desk and handed me a pen. "Here's your boarding contract. Let's make it official."

Real arrived at Centerline Farm two days later, and

I went there every day that Al wasn't home. I rode, watched lessons, talked to Bonnie and Susan, and watched Layne ride the training horses. I brought a lunch and ate on the patio or in the observation room. My days were full, and I slept soundly, with or without Al.

18 - CYRA

After he kissed me on the cheek and squeezed my shoulder, I watched Al leave the barn. Then I turned and watched Cyra as she walked out of the tackroom with a handful of horse treats.

Cyra gave several treats to her mare, who was bluish-grey with a small diamond shaped star on her forehead. She had a thick black mane and tail and black legs with a bit of feathering along the legs and pasterns. The mare's forelock was thick and hung down between her ears. It covered her eyes and was so long it almost touched her nose. When she moved her head to take the cookies from Cyra's hand, her forelock danced, and her eyes sparkled underneath it.

"Good girl!" Cyra patted her and led the mare into her stall. She closed the stall door, then turned and saw me watching her. She walked over to me and Real.

"May I?" She showed me the remaining treats in her hand.

"Sure," I said. "He loves them."

Cyra put the treats under Real's nose, and he took them from her hand, chewing each one before reaching with his lips for the next one. Cyra laughed. "He's a polite one!"

I smiled, "He was advertised as a real gentleman

and he is, so I gave him the barn name Real." I was embarrassed the minute the words left my mouth. I felt my face grow warm and thought, "What a babbling fool I am!"

But Cyra didn't seem to notice my embarrassment. "What's your level?" she asked, then added, "Sorry, I'm Cyra. I've seen you around."

"Hi. I'm Marsha. I've shown Training and First Level. I've schooled second. I rode schoolmasters at Greenwood when I was younger. Your mare is beautiful, I've watched you ride and you're a good rider." I stopped to catch my breath.

"Cool and thanks," Cyra said. "So, was that your husband? He doesn't know much about horses, does he?"

"Yes, he's my husband and no, he doesn't know much about horses. He's a lawyer, and he works a lot. He's hardly ever home. I was bored, so I got back into horses, and, well, here I am. Real and I have been her a couple of weeks."

It was easy to babble on to Cyra. She paid complete attention while I spoke, and her blackened eyes never left my face. She smiled and nodded and raised her eyebrows as I talked, so I continued, "Real has been trained through 4th Level, and I hope to start showing in June. He's a Dutch Warmblood. What's your mare's breed?"

"She's a Nokota. Her registered name is Chimalis. It means 'bluebird'." Cyra shrugged. "No one's heard of them around here, but it's a pretty cool breed. They're from the last band of totally wild horses out west. I got her there. Long story. Anyway, sorry to rush, but I gotta go to work." Cyra gave Real a pat and turned away.

"What do you do?" I asked.

Cyra turned to face me. "I'm a stripper." She said and stared at me as if she were daring me to say something bad.

"Oh." I stumbled over my words: "Well, that's... exciting!"

"Ha!" Cyra's face broke into a grin. "That's the nicest thing anyone here ever said about my job!"

"Well, I saw the movie 'Ladies of Burlesque'. It was based on a novel written by the stripper called Gypsy Rose. So, you go on stage, and everybody is fascinated, watching you. You're in control. You probably make them beg for more!"

"Yes, I do! And I love the way they drool!" Cyra laughed.

"I'd like to see you work," I said, not stopping to think. But, yes, I really wanted to see Cyra make her audience drool.

"Are you sure?" Cyra frowned and put her hand on her hip. "You don't look like the kind of person who goes to strip bars."

"Well, I haven't ever been to one, for sure, but I'd like to see you work. If you're half as good at stripping as you are at riding your horse, you've got to be good," I said truthfully.

And I meant it. Cyra was a treat to watch when she rode her mare. She sat straight and hardly moved. Her mare performed upper level movements effortlessly and Cyra looked as if she were a part of the mare's body as they practiced canter pirouettes and tempe changes. When Cyra was riding, you didn't notice the piercings or the hair. You saw only the horse and rider dancing together. You wouldn't notice the hair, anyway. At Centerline, everyone wore a helmet when riding in a lesson. It was Bonnie's rule.

"Okay, cool." Cyra smiled. "I'll take you with me someday, but not today. Gotta go! Nice to meet you," she added.

"Same here," I said.

Cyra turned and walked down the barn aisle and I watched as she disappeared from sight, heading to the parking lot. I wondered if Cyra also thought my husband had been flirting with her.

"Well ,there she goes! Off to thrill the crowds!"

I jumped as Layne's voice cut into my thoughts. She was leaning on the tackroom door. How long she had been there?

Layne was attractive, and always seemed friendly, but I couldn't relax when she was around. Maybe it was because I was taking lessons with her and felt slightly intimidated. I was anxious to do well in my lessons, and that was probably why I felt uneasy in her presence.

"Sorry I startled you," Layne said, smiling at me.

"I didn't know you were behind me."

"Sorry," Layne said. "It's these shoes." She lifted and turned one foot to show me the rubber sole on her shoe. "I scare the horses, too, sometimes. Maybe I should go back to my clogs. The way the wooden soles on my clogs clacked when I walked, I couldn't sneak up on a dead man!" She laughed at herself, and I forced myself to laugh too.

Without stopping to think about it, I asked: "Layne, what do you know about Cyra? She's an interesting person." I wasn't pretending. Cyra was interesting, and I certainly wanted to know more about her since my husband had also found her interesting.

"Cyra? You mean as a rider or as a person?"

"Both, actually."

"Well, I can tell you lots about Cyra, but it will take a while. How about taking a youngster out with me on a trail ride and we can talk?"

"Me? Ride one of the training horses? I don't know. I'm just an amateur." My heart gave a little jump.

"Nothing to it. They're tired from working earlier with me and Bonnie, and I just want to let them stretch and have a little fun. We will just walk and talk." Layne sauntered over to where I was standing, looked down at me and lifted her eyebrows. "You want to know more about Cyra? Follow me."

"Okay." I put Real in his stall with a flake of hay and then followed Layne down the aisle to the training horses' stalls. Maybe riding out with Layne and getting to know her better would make me feel more relaxed around her.

Layne took a tall chestnut gelding named Tempo and a short, black gelding named Rodney from their stalls.

"Rodney looks like a Quarter Horse," I said.

"Right, and Tempo looks like a giraffe!" Layne laughed. "Rodney is, in fact, a Quarter Horse and very lazy," Layne told me. "Tempo is a Hannoverian and tired, so we will just walk them and not worry about anything but the scenery and our gossip!"

I laughed and began to brush Rodney.

"Their saddles and bridles are in the tackroom with their names on them" Layne told me.

I put the brush down. "Okay."

I made two trips to the tackroom, grabbing the pads and saddles first, one under each arm, and handed them off to Layne, who put them on the horses and adjusted the girths. On my second trip for the bridles, I grabbed my helmet and my quilted vest, just in case the afternoon turned chilly. It was April in Michigan, and the weather could change quickly.

19 - TRAIL RIDE WITH LAYNE

Layne led Tempo down the aisle to the back of the barn, and Rodney and I followed them. We used a mounting block near the outdoor arena to climb aboard the horses and then walked down a path by the turnout paddocks.

"This path takes us to the edge of the state land," Layne told me, pointing ahead.

The path led to a well-groomed trail shaded by oak trees. From the size of the trees, I could see that they were very old. Their leaves made a canopy over the trail and allowed little sparkles of sunlight to slip through. Birch trees with their paper-like bark were growing near the oak trees.

"Beautiful trees," I said.

Layne pointed to one of the taller trees. "Take a look at that one. That's a shagbark hickory." The tree she pointed to was probably fifty feet tall, and its branches reached out to us. Large slabs of bark were peeling from the trunk of the tree.

"What's wrong with it? Is it diseased?"

"It's fine. That's the way it grows. It unfolds, I tell everyone. But don't feel silly. I thought the same thing when I first saw it. I had never seen a shagbark until I moved here from South Dakota. Cyra told me about it. She said Indians used the nuts for food and the lumber for their bows and for smoking meat. They say the nuts have a great flavor, but I've never eaten one. Cyra said it likes to grow near oak trees." Layne looked at me and shrugged.

"So, you're from South Dakota? What is dressage like in South Dakota?"

Layne laughed and said, "Dressage is pretty rare in the Dakotas, except for where I came from. I was lucky to live near Nisland, where Rivervale Farm is, in the western part of the state. I spent a lot of time there as a working student, taking lessons in dressage and jumping. After I graduated from high school, I apprenticed under Craig Heckert. He owns Rivervale. I went from training to Prix St. Georges with Craig."

"Wow. That's great," I said.

Layne frowned. "I would probably still be there if it wasn't for my husband and I'd probably have my gold metal by now."

"What brought you here?"

"My husband's work transferred us here a couple of years ago. I got the job at Centerline over the phone because of Craig. I didn't have to interview because Bonnie knows Craig, and she hired me when I called Centerline before we even moved here. Susan was upset with her for doing it that way, but it worked out."

"Lucky for Bonnie!" I laughed.

"Susan doesn't like me." Layne said.

"Really? What makes you think that?"

"She talks to me only if she has to, and she doesn't treat me like anything other than a worker."

"Well, you are an employee. Maybe she's just busy when you see her?" I couldn't imagine Susan being unfriendly.

"Maybe," Layne said.

We walked on and the trail gradually slopped down. Maple and poplar trees appeared. Wild ginger and bloodroot carpeted some areas and lupine and foxglove poked through the debris of fall and winter in others.

"This is beautiful," I said. "Thank you for showing it to me."

"I thought you hadn't been out here yet." Layne smiled. "Everyone loves this path. We use it to cool out the horses, or ourselves, sometimes!" She laughed and said, "We are lucky. Not many stables have great trainers, good footing and beautiful state land to ride out on."

"Not to mention excellent boarders!" I added, laughing.

"Right," Layne agreed with me.

I decided to let Layne know how she affected me. I took a deep breath, and told her, "Most of the time I've been around you, I felt nervous. Maybe it's because I take lessons from you. But now I feel a lot better, getting to know you, I mean."

Layne smiled. "I'm an okay person. But you've

probably heard that I lose my temper with working students? I can be quick to criticize, but I say my piece and it's over. If they don't get it then, and don't change, I'm done with them. I have no patience with people who won't do things the right way."

"Oh. I hope I don't do anything wrong. I want to stay on your good side, and in this barn." I felt my face get a little warm. I was nervous again.

Layne laughed. "You're okay. I was referring to the working students. I have a lot of trouble with them. It's hard to find good people nowadays."

"Oh. Well, the working students seem wonderful." I was confused.

"Yes. We have a good crew right now, but it took a while to get them. We usually take four, but we've had seven this year. The first one quit a few days after she started, saying she wanted to train and ride, not learn about daily care and maintenance. We tell all of them that they are here to learn everything, not just riding. That is only one part of the working student agreement."

"What does a working student learn?" I had been a working student, but I knew each barn ran a slightly different program.

"Well," Layne frowned a little, "we educate them on the different types of hay, the kinds of feeds, how to run a stable as a business, how to work safely with all ages of horses and people, and so on. Our point is that, even if they wind up as the 'trainer', they need to know the difference between good and bad care. It will make or break them as trainers or stable owners. They clean stalls, turnout horses, feed, water, medicate and bandage, change sheets and blankets - all the grunt work - in exchange for their education, riding lessons and a small salary. We, basically, have to teach them how to do everything because it's amazing what they don't know," she added.

"That sounds great," I said. "They would have to pay to learn all that in other places."

"That's right!" Layne nodded, "But kids nowadays want their parents to send them to a school to learn this stuff and get a certificate to hang on the wall. They are probably coddled all the way, too!"

I didn't know what to say. Layne was right. I knew a couple of lesson kids from my working student days whose parents sent them off to what I called horse college. When they graduated and tried to find jobs as trainers, they learned how the real world worked. It wasn't easy, and both quit.

"The second girl hung on for about a month," Layne said, "but she was lazy and wouldn't get all the work done. She thought her abilities were being wasted. I told her to leave. It was almost the same with the next two. I don't have a lot of faith in working students."

"I can imagine that they can be frustrating."

"All they want to do is ride the pretty horses. I tell them that we are a boarding and lesson barn and that people pay us to care for their horses so that they, not we, can ride them." Layne shook her head, and I could see that she was getting a little worked up.

I tried to calm her down and said, "Young girls probably ask you for a job all the time. What do you tell them?"

Layne sighed and said, "Most of them say, 'Hey, if you need some help, I can ride.' So I play along and ask them what they've ridden. It turns out that most of them have been on a friend's dead-broke horse and they think they can ride!" She shook her head and frowned again. "So I say, well, we have plenty of work to do around here. There's always lawn cutting, weed whacking, and cobwebs that need to come down. And then they go away."

"Sounds like you have your hands full," I said. "I don't know how you do it. I'm busy enough just trying to ride and stay out of everyone's way. I'm confused all the time!"

Layne laughed. "You'll settle in soon. You haven't met all the boarders and you haven't been to a show. The boarders are a great group of people and all of them, except Cyra, are financially secure." Layne winked at me when she said "financially secure."

"Cyra, well, she's different," I laughed. "But I like her." I surprised myself when I said that, but realized it was true. Cyra spoke openly about herself, and she had looked straight into my eyes. Yes, I liked her. She was honest.

"Yeah, she's got spunk. She came out of nowhere,

and she's made herself a really good rider. She has a good mare, and they have potential. If only she had money and family support."

"What's her story?" I didn't want to mention that Cyra had told me she took her clothes off to earn a living.

"Well, Cyra came here a couple of years ago with her mare. She came in a ragged truck, pulling a ragged horse trailer. But it wasn't even her truck and trailer. A guy who looked like a cowboy just dropped her off. She let him leave without even asking if we would board her horse!"

"Really?" I remembered my first day at Centerline and how I had worried that they wouldn't take me as a boarder.

"She said she was new in town and knew about the stable from articles in Dressage Today and Chronicle of the Horse magazines. We didn't think she could afford to board here, but she fooled us."

"She was dumped here by a cowboy?"

Layne laughed, "No, I don't think he dumped her. I think he was just her transport. Anyway, she showed us a current Coggins and shot record from Nevada, so we put the mare in a stall and brought out a boarding contract. She didn't blink at the monthly fees or the security deposit. Coughed it all up in cash. She's been here ever since and we have less trouble collecting from her than from most of our boarders."

I decided to play dumb. "What's her line of work?"

Layne looked at me and squinted her eyes. "Don't

play me. I heard her tell you she is a stripper. I didn't mean to eavesdrop, but I overheard your conversation. I was in Duke's stall. But I think she does more than strip, if you know what I mean?"

"What?"

"I mean she probably goes on dates for money, to put it politely. But that's her business. She doesn't cause me any problems, and she's a good rider. She flew through the lower levels and now she takes her lessons from Bonnie, not me. Bonnie loves teaching her, and she wants to take her to Florida, but that's a lot of money. And I don't think the women who go to Florida would like it, either!"

We came to a clearing with a stream, and both horses stopped. It was the stream Susan had pointed out to me on the map of the farm.

But my thoughts were still on Cyra. "What does she do for an instructor in the winter when Bonnie's gone?"

"I teach her. I've ridden the Grand Prix movements, and I've trained and shown thru Intermediare II, so I help her during the winter months. When she catches up with me, I guess we can teach each other!" Layne laughed.

"Wow. Will you be showing Grand Prix this season?"

Layne frowned. "No. Marlboro has a tendon injury. I'm sidelined until it heals."

"I'm sorry. How did it happen?"

"I don't know. He came in from the paddock with a little swelling and a limp. The vet said he tore the tendon in his right leg. He's on stall rest for six to eight months."

"That's awful."

"Yeah." Layne looked away.

There it was again. I had talked too much and found another sore spot with Layne.

I sighed and looked down at the water and watched it flow slowly southward. Rodney stretched his neck out and blew his nose.

Layne's horse started pawing, impatient to move on. She gathered her reins and said, "We can ride a little longer. Then we will have to go back. I have to do evening chores."

"Okay. Thank you for taking me out here. I can help you with chores when we get back."

Layne managed to smile. "Thanks." She turned her horse and led the way across the stream.

I followed her. Now I had a little more information on Cyra, I knew what to look out for if Al continued to show an interest in her.

Layne turned around in her saddle. "Follow me! I want to show you something."

We reached the other side of the stream and Layne dismounted. She plucked something out of the water, and handed it to me. Then she got back on Tempo.

It was a rock. It was dark blue, speckled with black. I was puzzled but slipped it in my vest pocket and walked Rodney out of the stream to catch up to Layne.

"What's with the rock? It's pretty, but..."

"You'll see in a minute."

"Oh. Okay." I couldn't imagine what we would do with a rock.

After leaving the stream, we entered a meadow full of dandelions and spring grasses. "Is this what you wanted to show me?"

"No, this is just a meadow. Follow me," Layne said, and kicked Tempo into a canter. He must have been tired because she had to pump her legs to get him going. I felt sorry for him and thought Layne looked like a cowgirl dressed in the wrong clothes.

I was forced to do the same with Rodney to follow her. On the other side of the meadow, we slowed to a trot and entered yet another shaded trail in the woods. Layne slowed her horse to a walk, and sighing with relief, I did the same.

A few minutes later, we came to a small circular clearing in the woods. In the middle of the clearing was a statue about three feet tall of an Indian girl, seated on the ground, holding a deer in her lap. The statue was surrounded by colorful rocks of all sizes, placed about six feet away in a circle around the statue.

"Hop off Rodney and step inside the ring of rocks. Tell the statue your troubles," Layne said. "Then place your rock in the ring and leave your trouble behind. That's the story I was told."

"That's beautiful," I said. "The story, and the rocks and the statue. I've never seen anything like it."

"These are all river rocks," Layne said. "Rocks worn smooth by a river or stream like the one we just crossed."

"The rocks look like colorful eggs," I laughed. "Some are so small, they could be bird eggs, and some are so big, they could be dinosaur eggs!"

"Well," Layne said, "one day this was just a trail and the next day we found this clearing and the statue, surrounded by all these rocks. Someone put a lot of effort into this, and they did it all overnight."

I frowned. "Who did it?"

"No one knows. This is near state land, but there is no 'legend' on the statue, so we assumed that the state didn't put it here. It could have been anybody."

"But why? And how did they get it here? It looks heavy."

"They probably brought it and the rocks in by truck. There's a state road not very far from here. They could come in with a truck that way, although there isn't a real road. Just this trail."

"Oh," I said.

I slipped off Rodney and gave his reins to Layne. Then I stepped over the ring of rocks, and holding the rock Layne had given me, silently thought about Al and told the statue that I worried about his faithfulness. I felt a sudden urge to thank the statue, so I went closer and knelt down and placed my hand on the deer's head. I closed my eyes. "Thank you," I whispered to the statue. Then I took a deep breath and opened my eyes. I went to the ring of rocks and placed my rock in the ring with the others.

Layne popped her cell phone off her belt hook and said, "Time's up. We have to get back now. Just thought I'd show you the statue, and anyway, it was a good excuse to canter across the meadow. Let's do it again!"

Layne tossed Rodney's reins at me and turned Tempo, then cantered off down the trail. I shook my head and used one of the bigger rocks to climb back up on Rodney.

"Thank you for being a little horse," I said to him and stroked his neck. "I'm sorry you had to work again. This was supposed to be a walk for you, but I guess Layne forgot. I'll make it up to you when we get back to the barn." I wanted to give both horses a bath but knew they would have to settle for treats instead.

I turned Rodney around and asked him to trot. "I'm sorry, buddy," I told Rodney and scratched his withers.

Layne and Tempo were waiting for us at the edge of the meadow, but I didn't ask Rodney to canter. Layne would have to wait or go on alone.

Layne waved at us and let Tempo grab mouthfuls of grass while she waited.

Helping Layne with the evening chores was easy

because it was the work I had done in my youth. Grain, water, hay and sweep. Each horse had their own labeled bucket of grain previously made up, with supplements and medications added, so it was easy to feed by matching the horse's stall name plate to the name on the feed buckets. After that, I topped off water buckets while Layne prepared the feed buckets for the morning.

Standing outside each stall with the hose, filling water buckets, I was able to pause and study each horse. I was starting to learn their personalities and their physical characteristics. Soon I would be able to recognize and name each one outside of their stalls.

As I watered Chimmy, I told her, "I'm getting to know your owner. She is an interesting person!" Chimmy looked up from her hay and blew softly on my hand. That made me smile.

I thought that helping Layne would make me feel more comfortable around her. It would certainly help me become familiar with the barn. In the two weeks I had been there, I still hadn't met all the owners, and knew only half of the horse's names. As I helped Layne, I tried to memorize the names of the owners that were engraved on the horse's name plaques on each stall.

After she refilled the grain buckets, Layne started putting stable sheets on the horses. "Most owners don't put stable sheets on their horses but just leave them on the blanket bars. I usually put them on at night, unless it's too hot. I just can't see them laying down in a poop pile without a sheet to keep them clean!"

"Do you put sheets on all the horses?"

"All but the broodmares."

"That's a lot of sheets!"

"Yep. I put sheets on Bonnie's horses too. You would think she would do her own horses, but no, she leaves me to do it."

"How many horses does Bonnie own?" I asked.

"Two. The broodmares and foals are owned by the farm. You saw her ride Bravo today. She owns a youngster named Zenith. He's a four-year-old and just started under saddle. I've been riding him since March."

"Wow! You're training Bonnie's young horse?"

"Well, I wouldn't say I'm training him," Layne frowned. "I'm just putting some time on him. Riding him so that he can carry a rider with confidence and go forward. There are always a few spooks and bucks. Just young horse things. We don't want Bonnie to ride through those," Layne said with a grin. "She's too valuable to the farm to get hurt!"

"Well, I would think that you are, too." I frowned. "Bonnie couldn't manage the farm without you."

"Oh yes, she can. A Grand Prix trainer like Bonnie will always attract ambitious young trainers. Anyway, she will have to do without me some day, hopefully soon, because I plan to have my own place," Layne added.

"And your boarders will receive excellent care for

their horses, from what I can see," I said.

Layne stopped and put her hands on her hips and frowned. "Most of the boarders don't even know what we do for them. They expect us to do everything we do, but they don't know exactly what we do, or how long it takes." Layne shrugged, "That's just the way it is here, I guess. But, at my farm, I'll make sure they know!"

"Well, I know now, and I thank you." I replied. "And thank you for the trail ride. It was a lot of fun, and I really liked the little shrine with the deer. Maybe someday we will find out who placed it there. Anyway, thank you. I had fun."

"I'm not so bad, huh?" Layne said and winked at me.

20 - IRENE

Friday and Saturday came and went without a word from Al. On Sunday I arrived at the stable at 11 am for a lesson with Layne and afterward ate lunch, sitting alone in the patio area in front of the barn. It was serene, eating and listening to the muffled sounds of the horses in their paddocks. I could hear them snorting and the friskier ones romping in the cool, crisp spring air.

After lunch, I watched Bonnie ride her Grand Prix horse, Bravo, and after that, Layne and I watched her give a lesson to one of the advanced students, a woman named Irene.

Irene was a poised but stiff rider. She held her shoulders back and her hands in the correct position, but they weren't flexible or giving hands. Bonnie was working on softening her hands so that her horse could move with more freedom in his gaits.

Her horse, a bay with four perfectly matched white stockings and an oval star placed exactly in the middle of his forehead, was named Parcel. He was quiet and obedient. His only protest, as far as I could tell, was an irritated flick of his tail when Irene jabbed him with her spurs when she failed to achieve a canter transition, trot extension, or pirouette, or whatever she was trying to get at the moment.

When the lesson ended, Parcel was steaming, and foam dripped off his neck and between his thighs. Irene dismounted and Layne and I walked into the arena. Irene handed Parcel's reins to Layne and removed her gloves. "See that he is properly cooled out," she told her.

"Will do," Layne responded, and winked at me.

Irene stalked out of the arena, down the aisle and out the barn door. We heard her Maserati fire up and leave the parking lot. She was gone.

Layne called over Meghan, one of the working students who was cleaning a stall near the arena. She handed her Parcel's reins. "Walk him in the arena until his breathing returns to normal, then bathe him and walk him a bit more. Then you can put him in his stall with hay. Put a cooler on him, and when he is dry, remove the cooler and put his day sheet on."

Meghan nodded and walked Parcel around in a big circle in the arena.

Layne watched as Meghan walked Parcel. "Irene's a retired model," she told me.

"That explains her aloofness, I guess, but why did she retire?"

"I never asked her," Layne said, "but I think it's because she married money, and she doesn't have to work anymore."

I stopped breathing. Maybe that's what people think about me. That I married money.

Layne interrupted my thoughts, "I should have done that. My husband is just a laborer. He works in construction. He promised me he would build me a barn, but now he's not interested. He says it's too much money and too much work."

"I don't think I would want a barn. It is a full-time commitment. And I agree with your husband. It's a lot of work." I remembered all the chores I did as a teenager on only five days a week. Boarding stables are 7 days a week, 365 days a year operations, and I didn't know anything about the finances of a barn and how to make it work as a business.

"Well, it's all I've ever done, and it's all I've ever wanted."

"I admire you," I said to Layne. "I don't think I could do it."

"You just need the right partner. Susan had her Aunt Nellie, and then her husband. Irene has the money to do it, but no interest in running a barn. She spends her days with horses and shopping."

"Maybe she shouldn't have retired. How old is she?"

"Irene's in her late twenties, but I think she was ready to retire. She never talks about modeling."

I turned to Layne. "She's kind of a prima-donna, isn't she? Or maybe she's just not happy." Was that why Irene was so aloof? Did she give up her career for money, and then realize she made a mistake?

Money was never a factor when I married Al. In fact,

I was surprised that he wanted me to quit working after we got married.

Layne shifted her weight from one foot to another. "She's not as snotty as she acts. Like for Christmas and my birthday, she gives me a big cash present."

I was doubtful. Generosity with money did not make a person less of a snot, I thought.

I pushed myself away from the arena rail. "Well, it's getting late. I've got some errands to run before I head home."

"See you tomorrow," Layne said.

21 - HOME

On the way home, I stopped in Richmond and said a brief hi to my mother. She was at work, as usual. Her only day off was Wednesday. She was serving dinner at the restaurant she had worked at for the last fifteen years, and I had only a few minutes to give her a kiss and say hi before she had to rush off, but it was good to see her and it made me smile.

Driving home in semi-darkness, and thinking about the day, I sighed. My route home took me onto I-94, heading back into the city of Grosse Pointe. Known for old money, security, culture and civility, it could not give me the peace and fulfillment I felt while I was at Centerline Farm.

I drove slowly down my street. It was dusk and the street lights were coming on. Houses were lit up and I could see people inside them. The lights had come on at my house too, due to automatic timers, but I knew it was empty. I drove my car up to the garage door, which opened automatically. I drove into my side of the garage and the garage door closed behind me.

I got out of my car and looked at the empty space where Al parked his car when he was home. My car door bumped up against my leg as if to remind me to shut it. I turned and shut the door and listened to the soft, clicking sound it made as it closed.

I walked through the half empty garage and my paddock boots made soft one-two sounds as my heel, then the front of my foot touched the ground.

Opening the door to the house produced a small push of air against my face as the air in the house equalized with the air in the garage. I closed the door to the half-empty space behind me and took my boots off in the mudroom. Then my riding clothes followed. I pulled on a fluffy white bathrobe and left everything horse-related in the mudroom, leaving the smell of my Real world behind.

On my way to the shower, I walked into the kitchen on my left. It was a large kitchen with a marble surfaced island in the center. Cutlery stood in slots on the right side of the island, and pots and pans hung above it. The kitchen had a commercial size refrigerator, a double oven for baking or broiling meats, and a 48 inch range top.

Cabinets holding spices of every variety were on the left of the cooking area and dishes for everyday use were in cabinets to the right. The "good" dishes were stored in an ornate cabinet in the formal dining room, which had an entrance from the living room. The kitchen also had a pocket door which opened into the dining room, making it easy to serve dinner guests.

There was a breakfast nook in one corner of the kitchen and a serving bar with tall chairs lined the length opposite the ovens and refrigerator. A half-wall behind the serving bar separated the entertainment area from the kitchen.

The entertainment area had a large L-shaped couch, two over-stuffed lounge chairs, a pool table, a bar, and a wall covered by a flat screen TV.

Sliding glass doors led to a covered patio big enough for 20 people to stand or sit comfortably in. At the end of the patio was a large in-ground pool, two dressing rooms with showers, a full size, fully stocked bar, and a custom-built stone pizza oven and barbecue grill. The surrounding lawn, trees and flowers were groomed weekly by a gardening service.

Sometimes I thought my home was big enough to host the entire village, but it was seldom used. Most of the time, I felt embarrassed by my unused wealth. At other times, I felt like a guest in my own house.

I peeked into the formal dining room and looked at the oversized polished wood table. It was flanked by cabinets on one wall and a bar on the other. Heavy drapes were closed over the windows, and the room seemed to be wrapped in silence. I paused at the door as if a membrane were separating me from the contents of the room.

I turned away and entered the living room, walking on the thick carpet with my bare feet. The carpet felt soft, and I wiggled my toes into it. The dent I created sprang back as soon as I walked away, leaving no trace of my steps. I moved on to the couch and touched the upholstery, which was as soft as a well-groomed horse.

It reminded me of Real's muzzle.

The silence of the living room pressed on my ears.

Maybe I should get a dog, I thought. Then there would be noise and a living thing in the house. But no, I decided quickly. Al would be gone, and I would be at the barn too much to have a dog. It would be lonely.

With a sigh, I turned and headed to the master bedroom. It was also encased in silence. Drapes and thick walls sealed the room from outside noises, but a bedroom lamp, operated by a timer, was on. The lamp's warm glow welcomed me into the room.

The master bedroom was large. In fact, my mother's apartment was the same square footage as the master bedroom, and that always made me feel guilty. If it were earlier in the day, I would call her, but she went to bed early, right after her dinner shift at the restaurant, and I didn't want to wake her. I would call her tomorrow or stop by the restaurant again.

My mother lived alone in the city of Richmond in a small apartment above a garage. She had a cat, Miss Priss, and an aquarium of fish to keep her company.

I liked cats, but not in the house. I liked fish too, but they required a lot of work and tended to die on me, anyway. My mother, on the other hand, had great luck with tropical and saltwater fish, and the many cats she had owned never slept on her head or woke her at 5 am, as they did with me when I was a young girl.

My mother had come to see Real once during the last two weeks and seemed to enjoy watching me groom and ride him for her. She spent a lot of time talking to Susan that day, and I think they enjoyed each other.

I have to spend more time with Mom, I thought. I had been avoiding that because, during our last visit on her weekly day off, she had asked, in her straight-forward way, "Marsha, is everything all right with you and Al?" I assured her that it was, but I didn't think she believed me. I would talk to her soon, but I just wanted to think about things first.

I decided to soak in the hot tub instead of taking a shower and gathered some candles and a book. When the tub was full, I slipped in and reached for my book, but jumped when my cell phone rang. I put the book down and picked up my phone. It was Al.

"Hi, Hon! I finally got back to the hotel at a decent hour so I could call you. How are you doing?"

"Fine. I just got in, myself. Where are you? You didn't tell me where you were going."

"I didn't? I'm sorry, and I'm sorry for not calling you the last two nights. Our team has been working past midnight on this case. I didn't want to call you that late."

"I understand."

"We are in Texas," Al said. "It looks like we might not have to go to trial. We meet again in the morning, and we hope to settle. It's a rape case. A rich young man from Detroit is accused of raping a young man in Texas."

"How awful. Is your client innocent?"

"Our clients are always innocent," Al laughed. "They are until proven guilty. Remember?"

"Well, that must be a little hard for you sometimes. I know we haven't talked about it before, but how can you defend someone you know is guilty?"

"I didn't say that. We don't talk about guilt. Our job is to prove innocence, or at least produce a just cause. We never ask our client if they are guilty."

"Um, I don't think I could do your job. No, I couldn't do it. The poor girl's family."

"It was a guy," Al corrected me.

"Your client is a woman accused of rape?" I was stunned.

"No, I didn't say that. Our client is a rich young man who is accused of rape. Of a poor young man. It looks like a lawsuit for a large amount of money. And I shouldn't even talk about it. I'd better get off the phone. We have a meeting early tomorrow morning. I just wanted to call you before I go to bed."

"Okay, I miss you," I said. "Get some rest."

"I will try to call again tomorrow to let you know whether we will come home tomorrow or stay here a bit longer. We are hoping to settle out of court. I'll buy you a new saddle when I get back," Al joked.

"Just come home soon. I miss you."

"I miss you too. You take care. Don't fall off that horse. I don't want to have to sue anyone!" Al chuckled.

"Don't talk like that, Al! Anyway, Michigan is a no-fault state when it comes to horses, remember?"

I smiled. Maybe he didn't know?

"Just kidding," Al said. "Good night, honey."

"Good night. I love you."

"I loved you first," Al said and made me laugh.

I felt a little better. I slid down in the tub and opened my book. For the next hour, I read about Anky Van Grunsven who won nine World Cups, three Olympic gold medals and two World Championships. Anky was another tall, skinny blonde like Bonnie.

When I compared myself to Anky and Bonnie, I felt like a common farm girl next to their beauty. I couldn't compare myself favorably to Layne or even the dark-haired Irene, who, even though she was almost thirty, was thin and elegant, with a flawless, tanned complexion.

I got out of the tub, dried myself and stood on the scale. At five feet two inches tall and weighing 127 pounds, I was "ideal" in weight, according to a chart I found on the internet, but the mirror told me something else. I had a bulge around my waist, well-padded hips, and a layer of fat on my belly. Certainly, less than ideal. I had been thin for my wedding. Maybe it was time for a weight loss and exercise program.

I went to bed determined to lose weight and look more like the horsewomen I admired. And maybe I would lighten my hair, too.

22 - GETTING TO KNOW CYRA

I walked into Centerline's restroom in time to see Irene turn at the waist and admire her new riding pants in the full-length mirror. Her pants were light brown with a full leather seat in dark brown. Slanted pockets at the waist accented her long, thin frame.

Irene didn't seem embarrassed when I caught her looking at her backside in the mirror. She turned slowly around with a smirk on her mouth that seemed to say, "Top that!" But her smirk changed quickly to a frown.

"Not too bad looking for an OLD butt!" someone behind me said.

I turned around and saw that Cyra had walked into the restroom behind me.

"And YOU can kiss it!" Irene hissed at Cyra and swept by, pushing Cyra aside as she shoved her way through to the door.

"Bitch!" Cyra called after her.

"You two don't like each other, do you?" I couldn't stop myself from laughing.

Cyra looked at me. She was wearing black riding pants and a red polo shirt. Her eyes weren't blackened, and she had no jewelry on. Her hair was brushed back in a short, boyish style. She had a hardened, angry look on her face when she turned to look at me. Her face slowly softened to a hint of a smile. "That's an understatement," she said.

"Oh," I said, "You look... normal!"

Then Cyra had to laugh. She put her left hand on her hip and extended her neck to me. "That's what I like about you! You are totally open and honest!"

"Well, not really. I have thoughts I keep to myself," I said, thinking about my husband and Layne's hint about Cyra's "side" work.

"Keeping something to yourself isn't dishonest," Cyra told me, "it's smart!"

I felt the need to change the subject and asked, "Are you just riding or taking a lesson today?"

"A lesson. I take a lesson every Monday and Friday."

"I like to watch you ride. I watched you on Friday." I paused and looked closely at Cyra. "You don't mind if I watch, do you?"

Cyra laughed. "I never mind an audience!" she said, and I had to laugh too because I knew she was referring to her work as a stripper.

Cyra started her warm-up with ten minutes of walk on a long rein. Then she trotted, first on a long rein, then gradually shortened the reins until the mare had a gracefully curved neck and an elastic connection to Cyra's hand. Soon they were circling and then making a serpentine figure in the arena. Next came transitions between gaits: walk to trot, trot to walk, walk to canter, canter to trot, canter to walk. After that, Cyra relaxed

Chimmy by walking on a long rein as she waited for instructions from Bonnie.

Bonnie entered the arena after Cyra had warmed up Chimmy. I noticed that she was wearing olive green full-seat breeches, a cream-colored long sleeved polo shirt and black boots with small, rounded spurs. Her long blonde hair was gathered and banded at the back of her neck. She was model-thin with long legs and an erect posture, attributes that I knew were ideal for a dressage rider.

Bonnie nodded "Hi" to me. I was standing by the arena rail, resting my forearms on it. At the same time, Layne walked up and stood by my side. I turned my head to watch Cyra and her mare, and jumped a little when I saw Layne right next to me.

"Oh! I didn't hear you walk up," I said.

"I'm sorry. It's these shoes! I have to put taps on them or something!" She laughed and shook her head as she watched Cyra.

I looked at Layne, doubting her words. I thought she enjoyed the element of surprise or the ability to be around the corner undetected. I decided, thinking of how Susan watched horses and people, to watch Layne in the future.

Bonnie began the lesson with Cyra, speaking in an encouraging manner. "There now, good, good. Yes! Good. Now half-halt to bring the hind legs under more. Good. Transition to walk, then canter. Yes. Good. Half pirouette at B. Easy, not too fast. Give her time. Yes.

Good. Now on to H, diagonal and flying change at X on to B, half-halt, prepare for a half pirouette at E." Bonnie's voice was low, and it had a surprising, almost masculine tone. She didn't have the light, feminine voice she used in everyday conversation.

"Where did Bonnie get that tone of voice?" I asked Layne.

"You noticed her accent? Well, maybe it really isn't an accent, but a way of thinking and speaking. She rode and studied in Europe, especially in Germany and Sweden. And she spent some time at the Spanish Riding School, too. I guess her voice is a blend of all that." Layne smiled. "Her physical training is, for sure. The way she walks, kind of hips first like a model, but not strutting like a model, but straight like a soldier? That's probably from the Spanish Riding School. But if she says 'Ya, ya, gut!' that's from Germany or Sweden!"

I cut my eyes to Layne and saw Layne looking at me with a grin on her face. I realized that Layne was making a joke and I laughed quietly. Layne's grin broadened.

"Have you studied abroad? Did you go to Germany or..." my voice died off when she saw Layne's eyes flicker and darken.

"That's my next stop, I guess. Divorce my husband and go," Layne said quietly. "Unless I get my own farm first."

"You really want a farm, don't you?"

"Sure. I'd rather be my own boss and do things the

way I want them. I don't want to be told what to do and how to do it." Layne was frowning and staring into the distance. "I have something in the works. But, if I don't get a farm soon, I will have to go to Europe, or just settle for always being small-time." She turned her head away slightly, and I saw the ligaments in her jaw tighten as she gritted her teeth.

I was thinking about how much passion Layne must have for her dream when Irene strolled up and stood by Layne. Irene watched the lesson for a few minutes and then said, "The bitch is good."

"Yeah. Cyra is too," Layne shot back. Irene and Layne grinned, made a fist and knocked them together.

I was beginning to see another side to Layne. People are complex, I reminded myself. And she's the assistant trainer. She has to get along with everyone. I turned my attention back to the lesson.

Layne and Irene mumbled together for a while and then Layne turned to me. "We're going for lunch. Want to come?"

"No, I need to watch and learn all I can," I smiled at her and glanced at Irene, who was looking down the aisle with a manicured hand on her hip, as if posing for a photographer.

At the end of the lesson, Cyra kicked her feet out of her stirrups and dropped the reins, letting her mare walk freely around the arena. Chimmy dropped her head and walked in a slow tempo with her head low.

She seemed relaxed and happy. I waited for Cyra and opened the arena gate when she pointed Chimmy in my direction.

"I enjoyed your lesson," I told her.

Cyra jumped off Chimmy. "I saw you had company. I wish you had a recorder so I could have a good laugh at what was said!"

"Well, I didn't hear much," I admitted. "They were talking to each other, not to me."

Cyra nodded and smiled. Her eyes slid toward me. "Maybe you should watch who you hang with. You don't want people getting the wrong impression."

"I'm not hanging with Irene, if that's what you mean. I can tell you right now, I don't like her!" I said emphatically.

Cyra laughed. "No, I meant me! If you hang around me, like now, people might get the wrong idea."

"That's their problem, isn't it? I don't like a lot of things about Irene, and I am disappointed that Layne is so cozy with her, but that's her choice, not mine."

Cyra smiled. "You're for real, aren't you?" She took off her helmet and shook her head, then ran her hands through her hair in an attempt to comb it back.

"You look pretty real, yourself! Did you dress down for Bonnie and your lesson?"

"No, I don't have to work today, and I need to run some errands. I don't want to draw a lot of attention. The makeup and piercings are sort of my costume. For my job, you know, but sometimes I wear all that stuff to keep people away from me. It gets their attention, freaks them out, and they stay away."

"Oh!" I said, "Well, after you put Chimmy away, do you want to grab some lunch before you run your errands?"

Cyra looked at me. Hard. I thought she was going to say no, but she finally said, "Sure."

We decided to have lunch at a Mexican restaurant near the barn. Layne had told me about it, and I was eager to try it. Cyra was agreeable.

I drove. Cyra wasn't much of a talker, so we rode in silence, but it didn't make me uncomfortable since I was accustomed to so much silence at home.

At the restaurant, Cyra stepped out of the car and picked up a small stone in the parking lot. It was grey with black oval rings on it and was shaped like an egg.

Cyra showed me the rock. "It's a river rock," she said and pocketed it.

"I saw some river rocks, just the other day, at the clearing in the woods," I said. "You know, the one with the statue? Layne took me on a trail ride and showed me the statue and the rocks."

Cyra looked at me. "What do you think of the statue?"

"It's beautiful! Layne said no one knows who put it there. She said the clearing, the statue and the rocks just appeared one day!"

Cyra smiled and her eyes twinkled mischievously.

"It's a mystery!" she said.

The restaurant was housed in the same building as a convenience store. They were separated by a wall, shared a common restroom and probably had the same owner. The restaurant was informal and clean, and the food was, according to Layne, excellent.

Once seated, we ordered some appetizers and beef tacos. Cyra ordered coffee and water, but I decided to try the Mexican tea.

"How is the tea?" Cyra asked when I sipped it.

"Okay. Kind of heavy. Want to try it?" I pushed my cup of tea toward her.

Cyra raised her eyebrows, hesitated, then reached for the cup. "Ugh," she said, after tasting it. "I see what you mean!"

I laughed. "So, you're not working tonight?"

"No, it's Monday. The lechers are home being good boys after their weekend of partying!"

"I see. Well, if you don't mind me asking, what are your errands? Laundry and grocery shopping?"

"Not today. I have to open a savings account and enroll in a class for the summer session. It goes from the first week in May and ends the 2nd week in June. Just in time for the first horse show of the season."

"Oh! What class? Something fun?"

"No," Cyra smiled. "Just finishing my associate's degree. One more class to go. It's an elective, just to fulfill my credit requirements, and I really don't know what to take."

"Well, take something you like," I suggested.

"I like horses."

"How about an art class? Or a computer class? Or maybe a class in history?"

After a moment, Cyra said, "Come with me and help me choose?"

I hesitated only a second. What the heck, I had lots of time. "Okay, I will, and if I like the class, I'll sign up too!"

Cyra grinned. "Cool," she said.

We stopped at the bank first and were taken into a private office, where Cyra opened a savings and a checking account. When she finished filling out the paperwork, Cyra reached into her bag and pulled out a bundle of cash. She put it on top of the paperwork and pushed it over to the male bank clerk. "How much do you want in each account?" he asked.

"$5,000 in savings and $2,000 in checking," Cyra said.

The bank clerk looked over the paperwork and pushed one of the papers back to Cyra. "You might want to name a second person on your account, just in case you need them to make a withdrawal, write a check for you, or some other reason." He pointed to the bottom of the page. "Just fill in this part with their name, address and the other information."

Cyra took the paperwork back, pressed her lips together and sighed, staring into space for a moment.

She sighed again and bowed her head to the paper, writing. Then she pushed it back to the clerk.

He looked it over. "Okay. That looks good," he said and took everything to a bank teller to finish the transaction.

"That was hard," Cyra said. "I named my sister, but I really didn't want to. I don't like her much."

"I'm sorry," I said.

"Nothing you did," Cyra replied as the clerk came back. He handed Cyra her copy of the paperwork and a book of checks, explaining that they were temporary checks, good to use if she needed money before her regular checks came from the printer. Cyra gave them back to him. "Throw them away," she said. "I won't be needing them."

The clerk shrugged and said, "Okay."

As we left the bank, I said, "You must have a big goal in mind if you don't plan to touch the cash you deposited."

Cyra slid her eyes to mine and smiled. "Chimmy and I are going to Florida and train with Bonnie next winter."

"Oh wow, that's great! Good for you!" I said and thought it would certainly surprise Layne and irritate Irene.

Next, we went to the community college and looked at the classes available. After a little debate over life drawing, calligraphy and pottery, Cyra and I signed up for the pottery class. It met once a week on Mondays from 12 to 3 pm, so it wouldn't interfere with Cyra's job or take much time away from the barn. And, as I pointed out, "It can't be that hard, and we can actually use what we make in the class."

When they got back to the barn, Cyra said, "Thanks for the afternoon and signing up for a class. It was fun, but I have to run now. I have a date."

"I had fun too," I told her. "Take care."

"Watch who you hang with!" Cyra joked.

I laughed. "Have fun on your date," I said, and Cyra just looked at me, which made me wonder what kind of date she was going on.

I headed for home, thinking about Cyra's date. Then I thought about what Cyra had said: Watch who you hang with, and I wondered, am I hanging with Cyra to watch her because of Al, or do I really like her?

By the time I arrived at home, I had decided that I really liked Cyra. She seemed honest and tough, brave and talented. Yes, I liked her. But it didn't hurt to watch her, either.

23 - LUNCH AND SHOPPING

Al came home that evening. He walked in the door five minutes after I emerged from the shower, wrapped in my white bathrobe, my hair turbaned in a towel.

"Hi!" I said.

"Hi." Al walked over and gave me a hug.

I hugged him back, then pushed him to arm's length. "You look tired."

"I'm beat," he admitted. "Is there anything to eat?"

"I'll put some clothes on and make something for us. It won't take long."

"Okay. I'll be in the office. I have a couple of calls I need to make."

I changed into cargo shorts and a t-shirt and made a salad. I washed three varieties of lettuce, tore them into bite size-pieces, chopped tomatoes and sliced a bit of red onion and cucumber. I added crumbled feta cheese and added a few black olives. I placed it on the serving bar with a bottle of Greek salad dressing. Next, I took some sliced veal and lemons from the refrigerator and started water heating for noodles. Soon, dinner was ready, and Al and I sat down to eat in the breakfast nook in the kitchen.

We ate in silence. I knew Al was still thinking about his work, and I knew he couldn't talk about it.

When he finished eating, Al said, "Dinner was great, but I'm beat. I'm going to bed now. I have an early start tomorrow. Goodnight." He kissed me on the cheek. "I love you," he said and was gone.

I sat at the table and drank coffee. I looked at the empty plates and then at my hands. My nails were unpainted, and I needed a manicure. With a sigh, I picked up the dishes, rinsed them off and put them in the dishwasher.

Then I poured myself another cup of coffee and took it to the living room where I curled up with a book about Arthur Kottas and his method of training horses. I wondered how it would feel to be so talented with horses that you became the youngest head rider of the Spanish Riding School in its 400 year history.

I woke up when Al took the book from my hands. He was dressed in a dark grey suit and smelled like aftershave.

"Good morning. Next time, sleep in bed... with me," he said with a chuckle. "I have to go. See you tonight." Al kissed me on the forehead and turned to leave.

I struggled to wake up. "Uh... oh... what time will you be home?"

"I don't know. I have a meeting with a new client this afternoon. I will call you. Go to bed," he said, and he was gone.

I checked the time on my phone. It was 7 am. I had slept through the night on the couch. Nothing new.

With a sigh, I stood up and went to the kitchen to make coffee.

By the time I got to the barn, the horses had been fed and were munching on hay. Layne was removing their night sheets and getting them ready for turnout. "Hi Marsha!" she said brightly. "How are you today?"

"Fine. I fell asleep with Arthur Kottas last night!"

"Well, you keep good company," Layne laughed. "Are you going with us to the tack shop today?"

"Oh. I didn't know about it. Who's going?"

"Me, Irene, Bonnie, and anybody else who wants to go. We will get some lunch and shop until we drop. Come with us?" Layne laughed, "I'm sure you can find something you need!"

"Okay. I will. Do you want help with turnout?"

"Sure, it's a lot more fun with help," Layne said.

When the horses were ready, we led the first pair down the aisle. The horses' feet made a soft clip-clop, clip-clop sound as they walked down the barn aisle lined with rubber mats. They made almost no sound as we crossed the soft footing of the indoor arena on the way out to the paddocks behind the barn.

"Bonnie doesn't like me to take them through the arena, but she's not here yet, so we will cut through, just for today," Layne told me. "It's quicker."

I instantly felt guilty. I didn't like doing something Bonnie had asked Layne not to do. But I felt trapped and said nothing. We turned the horses out and headed back to the barn for two more.

I looked at the tracks we had made in the arena. "Horses hooves make peace signs."

"What?" Layne looked at me.

I felt a little silly but said, "Look at their hoofprints. It's a peace sign."

Layne looked down. "You're right!" she said. "I guess I never really looked at them that way before."

After the horses were turned out, Layne spent a few minutes talking to a young woman I didn't know. I glanced at them and went to pull Real out of his stall and tack him up. I had a lesson with Layne at 10 and I watched them as I groomed my horse. I was putting the saddle on Real when Layne finished her talk with the young woman and brought her over to me.

"Marsha, this is Kathie, our new working student."

"Pleased to meet you, Kathie." I held out my hand.

Kathie seemed a little reluctant but took my hand. Her hand felt limp and cold, like a dead fish.

Layne gave Kathie a nod and said, "You can help Mitchell with stalls. He volunteered to show you how we do things." Then she turned to me. "I'll meet you in the arena in ten minutes. Warm him up if you get there before me," and she turned on her heel and was gone.

Layne showed up at the indoor arena just as I had began trot serpentines, stretching Real's body through the curves and moving his rib cage side to side. After the serpentines, I cantered once around the arena in both directions, crossed the diagonal, trotted at X and walked at K. Then I stopped and waited for Layne.

"That was a good warm-up," Layne told me. "Now let's work on shoulder-in to haunches-in and do some turns on the haunches. We can end the lesson with a little work on canter-walk and play with flying changes."

After the lesson, Real was sweaty and needed to walk a bit before he was dry enough to be turned out. I removed his saddle and placed it on the arena rail. Layne leaned up against the rail and made small talk as I led Real round and round in the arena.

"Did you do anything exciting on the weekend?" she asked. "I went to the movies with Dave and made dinner for his friends on Sunday. It was a boring, waste of time weekend!" Layne laughed without joy.

"That was exciting compared to my weekend," I admitted. "I came to ride, but there were only a couple of boarders here and I hadn't met them yet. Bonnie was gone, and you were off, so I rode, grazed Real and went grocery shopping on Saturday. Then, on Sunday, I rode, grazed Real and went home to do the laundry on Sunday."

"You didn't do anything interesting with your husband?"

"No. He was in Pennsylvania, working on a case. I didn't see him until last night."

"What case? He's a lawyer, right?" Layne followed me as I led Real from the arena and put him in the aisle on crossties.

"Yes, but I don't really know what he's working on." I carried Real's saddle into the tackroom. I didn't want to talk about Al's work at the barn, but felt I had to say something. I stepped out of the tackroom and said, "He doesn't tell me. Lawyer-client stuff, you know. Not even the wife hears about it until it hits the newspapers."

"He gets written up in the newspapers?" Layne put her hands on her hips.

I started brushing the dried sweat off Real. "Not him. The cases, usually. He defends people accused of crimes. Mainly rich or famous people." I shrugged. "Sometimes he works on cases with his partners. They defend well-known or rich clients, so it usually makes the news."

"Then you hear about it?"

"Only what the newspapers write. And you never know if it's accurate." I tried to laugh. "He can't tell me anything, really. And I don't want to know. I can't imagine working for the people he defends..." my voice trailed off.

"You mean that they're usually guilty?"

"No. They are innocent until proven guilty. His firm always makes sure everyone knows that." I put my brush away. Then I threw Real's fly sheet over his back and buckled the chest straps, the belly straps and finally, the legs straps.

"Ready to go out? I'll grab Woody and we can walk them out together." Layne turned and went to get

Woody, Real's turnout buddy.

After the geldings were happily munching grass in their paddock, Layne and I went back to the barn just as Irene and Bonnie walked in. Irene was dressed in reddish-brown breeches, black paddock boots and a cream-colored cotton shirt with the collar turned up at the neck. Her long sleeves were folded up several inches to reveal a gold bracelet with a large yellow stone. Around her neck she wore a gold necklace with a matching yellow stone. She caught me looking at it. "Topaz," she said with an upward tilt of her head and turned to Layne. "Are you ready?"

"Yes, we are!" Layne declared and nodded toward me.

Irene's eyebrows shot up, but she said nothing.

"Marsha's gonna come with us." Layne told Irene and Bonnie.

"But, if you'd rather go alone, I understand," I said to all of them.

"Nonsense, you're coming with us to help stimulate the economy!" Bonnie smiled and walked up to me. "We'll go to lunch first," she said.

"Good, because I'm starving!" Layne said, laughing.

Irene sniffed, paired up with Layne and led the group to the parking lot where Susan was waiting for us with her van. I sat behind Susan and across from Bonnie after Layne and Irene claimed the back seats.

"Just like when we were kids, huh, Mom?" Bonnie said to Susan.

"Those were the days!" Susan smiled at me in the rearview mirror. "This van was packed every weekend with giggly teenage girls going to some horse event somewhere."

"We did a lot of things as a group when you ran the barn, Mom," Bonnie told her.

"Yes, the van feels kind of empty today, doesn't it?"

"Plenty of room for everything we will buy," Layne said to no one in particular.

"Mom won't let us part with this old van," Bonnie told me. "It comes in handy for barn outings and it's loaded with memories."

"I didn't know about the outings," I told Bonnie. "How many are there?"

"Oh, it's just casual, not planned or anything. A few of us get together for lunch and shopping now and then, like today. Sometimes we decide to audit a clinic, if we're not riding in it. Sometimes we go watch a show, if we're not showing. Nothing planned. It's just a kind of spur-of-the-moment thing," Bonnie explained.

"Oh. Well, maybe you could plan and schedule some outings in the future?" I suggested. "You could get a calendar and let everyone know in advance. It could make the barn feel more like a team. We had that kind of thing at my old barn when I was a teenager. We called ourselves the 'Centaurinas'. We went everywhere together. I think that's why we were so supportive of each other at the shows. We already had the team spirit before we got there."

Irene snorted and turned her head to the window, and I realized I was babbling again.

"That's a great idea!" Bonnie said. "I'll get a big wipe-off calendar and we can note interesting events coming up. Invite everyone to go as a group. Can I put you in charge of that? I'll give you dates for the events I know about, and maybe you can find a few more for us? I think that's a great idea!"

"Who, me? You want me to do that?" I looked at Bonnie.

"Yes, of course! It was your idea," Bonnie laughed. "Who would be better to do it? Will you do it?"

"Well, sure. I'd be glad to do it. But how will I find events for us to attend?" I was getting nervous.

"I know of a few coming up. Are you a member of MDA? Midwest Dressage Association? They post quite a few events. Then there are always events at area barns or veterinary clinics. They send us fliers. I'll pass them on to you. We could become a more active barn, with your help. I've been wanting to make us more united. This might be one way to do it." Bonnie smiled, and I sat back to think about my new "job" as the event coordinator at Centerline Farm.

In the middle seats, Irene sighed, and Layne cleared her throat.

"I think that's a wonderful idea," Susan looked at me in the rearview mirror and smiled.

I smiled back, but I felt a little uncomfortable. I was new at the barn and although I had met some of the boarders, I didn't know all of them. How would they feel about me scheduling events for them to attend?

I started thinking about the horses and boarders at Centerline. I knew most of the horses by then. I was familiar with the five horses in training and the three retired dressage horses who were used to give lessons to students without horses.

Layne owned a ten-year-old warmblood gelding called Marlboro, who she brought with her when she left South Dakota.

Irene owned a magnificent bay Hanoverian gelding named Parcel, and a four-year-old Westphalian gelding named Fortunate. Both were in training with Bonnie.

Meghan, one of the working students, owned a grey Arabian mare named Prakseda, nicknamed Proxy.

Gina owned Theodore, a leopard Appaloosa. Gina was a dressage rider who also rode on the trails and every year participated in the "Shore to Shore" ride sponsored by the Michigan Trail Riders Association.

Delores owned three German dressage ponies: Dimples, Squat and Mo. She was a dressage rider who bought the ponies for her granddaughters. They came weekly for lessons, but I hadn't met Delores. Layne said she was still in Arizona, where she spent most of her winters.

Connie owned two Quarter Horses. The larger gelding, she called Chance. He looked like a warmblood. The smaller gelding, who she called Zip, looked like a cowboy's horse. Connie was a short woman in her late 50's. She had owned horses all her life and had bowed legs to prove it. She had ridden cross-country and chased foxes in New England before moving to the Detroit area. In Michigan she learned to "event" but, when she got older, "and grew a brain," she told me, she took up dressage. Raising two daughters had a lot to do with it. She had to choose a safer sport and one that didn't carry the threat of broken bones. Her daughters didn't care for horses. They preferred fast cars and clean clothing, she said.

Danielle was a very thin and quiet sixteen-year-old who always wore one ear bud hooked to her iPod. She nodded at me when we were introduced, but her eyes had a faraway look, like she was thinking of something else. She owned a solid black Morgan called Woody short for Woodsman, who was Real's turnout buddy.

No one at the barn had bothered to introduce me to Cyra. And I had been at the barn a long time before Layne introduced me to Irene. I had the feeling that Layne didn't really want me to get to know Irene. That was okay by me. Irene was a snob.

I cleared my throat. "I don't think I can get all of your boarders united," I said. "It's such a diverse group."

Bonnie laughed, "Just make the calendar and those who want to join us, can. I know you will do a great job, and thank you for doing it!"

I nodded at Bonnie and smiled, but I wondered

what effect the calendar would have on Centerline's boarders.

Bonnie had already picked out a restaurant for our lunch. It was a newly opened Chinese restaurant in Oakland County called Chung's Cantonese Gardens. It was built with large white stones and had lots of glass windows. The parking lot was almost full. Susan had to park the van on the back side of the restaurant in the last row.

"Well," Bonnie said, "It's Tuesday, and they are packed for lunch! The review in the newspaper said the food is excellent, so it must be true. We may have to wait a bit, but we can have a drink at the bar if we have to wait."

"Absolutely!" Layne laughed. "I'm in favor of that!"

I was a little surprised but said nothing. My drink for lunch was coffee or tea, but I decided to go along with the crowd. I didn't want to be the odd one, and I wasn't driving.

Just as Bonnie predicted, we were asked to wait for a table. The hostess led us to the bar area, separated from the dining section of the restaurant by a short wall. We found a small table with two chairs and borrowed three more chairs from nearby tables. Seated as five at a table meant for two, put us in very close contact. Layne was pushed up against Irene and I squeezed between Layne and Bonnie. Susan was given the most generous space.

As soon as we were seated, we were greeted by an aproned male waiter. "Hi. What can I bring you, ladies?"

Susan spoke first. "I'll have light beer in a frosted mug," she said.

The waiter nodded and wrote on his pad, then looked at me.

Seeing the blank look on my face, Bonnie spoke up, "I'll have a frozen margarita, and bring one for her too." To me she said, "You'll love it!"

"Thanks," I said, relieved.

"What do you have in Chinese wines?" Irene asked the waiter, who was still writing on his pad.

He looked up and frowned. "Um, well, I don't know. I'll ask the bartender." The young man fumbled with his pad and grew red in the face.

"You do that," Irene told him coldly.

The waiter bowed his head and quickly left us.

"I didn't know China had wines!" Bonnie laughed.

"Oh, yes!" Layne leaned forward enthusiastically. "Irene and I visited a wine shop in Royal Oak and they have a whole section devoted to Chinese wines!"

Irene continued Layne's conversation. "It seems that China is determined to become one of the world's top wine producers. They import almost no wine but have over 400 wineries. And, considering that there are thousands of Chinese restaurants in the States alone, the investment potential is tremendous."

"Are you thinking of investing?" I asked her.

Irene seemed to stiffen a little. "Certainly not," she said. "I have other investments in mind."

"What other investments are you thinking about?" Bonnie asked. "I've only invested in horses!"

Irene examined her bracelet. "Nothing I can talk about at this time," she replied.

"Anyway," Layne quickly continued the wine conversation, "Dragon's Hollow produces a good Chardonnay and a good Riesling. Both are light and citrusy. They're not expensive and are really good wines!"

There was an awkward silence for a few moments, after Layne and Irene's information about Chinese wines. Fortunately, the waiter returned with two glasses of wine, a frosted mug of beer, and two frozen margaritas. He put the mug of beer in front of Susan, the margaritas in front of Bonnie and me and then, with a flourish of his right hand said, "Our very best Chinese wine, on the house!" and put them in front of Irene and Layne.

"Well, thank you!" Bonnie said to the waiter and lifted her glass in a toast. "Here's to a wonderful lunch and a very successful shopping trip!"

Susan, Layne, Irene and I touched our glasses to Bonnie's. "To a wonderful lunch and a very successful shopping trip," Layne repeated, and we laughed. After that, everyone seemed to relax, and soon we were led to a table.

I noticed that Bonnie left the waiter a tip, but no one

else did. I wondered if the drinks would be added to our food bill.

Lunch was excellent, just as the newspaper reviews had reported. We refused desert, but each of us grabbed a fortune cookie.

Bonnie held up her hand. "Wait!" she said. "Let's open them one at a time and read our fortunes out loud!"

"Okay, age before beauties," Susan said laughing and broke her cookie open. "You will seek change soon," she read out loud. "Yep, I'm getting the oil changed on the van while you girls shop!"

Bonnie read her fortune next. "You were born to lead."

"That's accurate," Susan said, laughing.

We seemed to be going in order of seating, so I read my fortune next. "Some have a good spirit, but others do not."

I looked at Susan and she winked at me.

Irene was next. "Fortune awaits those who seek it."

"That's accurate too," Bonnie said. "You will ride Fortunate soon!"

And Layne read, "Time is your friend."

"Is that accurate?" Bonnie asked her.

"Not so far," Layne replied, and I wondered what she meant.

After lunch, Susan drove us to the tack shop and left us there, saying she wanted to get a quick oil change on the van. Layne and Irene paired off, leaving Bonnie and me together.

"I need breeches, spur straps, and a new double bridle for Bravo. What do you need?" Bonnie asked.

"Probably everything," I laughed. "I'll follow you around and I'm sure I'll find lots of stuff I need!"

And I did. Bonnie recommended a set of fleece lined exercise boots and a Merino wool saddle pad for Real. For myself, I bought two DVDs on the "perfect position" in the saddle and a new pair of breeches.

When we left the shop and climbed into the van, Layne teased me. "Only one bag?" She and Irene had seven bags of clothing and tack between them and filled the back of Susan's van.

Bonnie and I put our purchases on the floor by our legs.

"What did you buy?" Bonnie asked Irene.

"Just some tack and clothes," Irene said vaguely.

"Well, you should model them for us!" Bonnie laughed, referring to Irene's former profession. "The clothes, I mean. Not the tack!" Bonnie said and laughed again.

I had been watching Irene's face and thought I saw a flicker of annoyance at Bonnie's joke. But then Irene said without smiling, "Certainly, but I charge!" and everyone laughed.

The ride back to Centerline seemed to take a long time. We rode mostly in silence, each of us thinking and watching the scenery pass by the van's windows.

24 - THE OUTINGS

True to her word, Bonnie bought an oversize wipe off calendar two days later and hung it on the wall outside the office. Then she found me brushing Real in his stall and handed me a stack of fliers and a couple of magazines. I had almost forgotten my promise to post events until I looked at her hands.

"Please find and post some interesting events for us?" she asked, handing me the bundle and a package of erasable markers.

"Oh, sure," I said, taking the bundle and markers from her.

"Thank you very much," Bonnie said. "I can't go through them with you because I have a lesson right now, but I'm sure you will find a few good ones in this bunch. And feel free to find others on your own."

"Okay. I will try," I said to Bonnie's back.

"Thanks again!" Bonnie said, turning her head to me as she rushed off.

She will be like Susan someday, I thought, smiling.

The first event I posted was a Musical Freestyle Clinic hosted by the Midwest Dressage Association. It was scheduled for the last Saturday in May. Susan added a note on the calendar that Bonnie would drive the van and leave the farm at 7:30 am. The clinic would be held at Michigan State in East Lansing and started at 9 am.

Seven people, including me, signed up. We had a final total of eight going, counting Bonnie.

On the morning of the clinic, Layne, Irene, Danielle, Connie, and the twins, Ben and Martin, were waiting with me in the parking lot. Bonnie brought Susan's van around to the parking lot at 7:10.

I had asked Cyra to join us, but she refused every time I mentioned it, so I was surprised to see her drive into the parking lot at 7:15. She stepped out of her little blue sedan, without make-up and piercing jewelry, but with a blanket slung over her shoulder.

"Cyra! You're going with us?" I asked.

Cyra nodded but didn't smile.

Regardless, I was delighted.

Irene was talking to Layne and had her back to the group but stiffened when I spoke. She turned abruptly.

"I'll drive my car. Layne can come with me. We've got a lot to talk about, anyway," Irene said and went to her car.

Layne shrugged at us and followed Irene.

Cyra and I sat at the back of the van and looked out the windows while Ben and Martin kept up a lively chatter with the rest of the group. Finally, I turned to Cyra and said, "What changed your mind?"

Cyra turned slowly from her window. "I came to the barn on a mission. So far, I've just been poking at it. I think I'm ready to dig a little deeper now," Cyra replied quietly, her eyes boring into mine.

Cyra's look gave me goose bumps. I rubbed my arms. "Well, that's great," I said. "Why so serious?"

"It's the most important thing in my life," Cyra said in a quiet voice and turned her head to look out the van window.

I stared at the back of Cyra's head. Somehow, it didn't seem that Cyra was talking about dressage. I shook my head. She had to be talking about dressage. That's all Cyra really cared about. But her mission should be making her happy. Not serious and sad. Maybe it was a do or die thing for Cyra? Maybe she was shooting for the Olympics, or at least a national championship.

I turned to look out the window and saw that it had begun to rain.

Even though it turned into a cold and rainy day, there was a large turnout for the clinic which was, fortunately, being held in the indoor arena. Cyra and I decided to stand near the gate where the demo riders entered, but soon we were chilled to the bone, and found seats so we could huddle under the blanket Cyra brought.

"How did you know to bring a blanket? The weather report said sunny and warm."

"I don't listen to the weather reports," Cyra said.

I nodded, but she hadn't answered my question. "Yeah, but how did you know?"

"I felt it in the air," Cyra said and smiled a little as she watched the next rider warm-up her horse.

"That's talent!" I joked.

Cyra slid her eyes to me but kept her face turned to the arena. "No, it's breeding," she said without a smile.

I wanted to laugh but couldn't. Cyra moved her eyes back to the rider and I thought, sometimes Cyra is strange.

When it was time for the lunch break, Cyra and I stayed seated to avoid the crowd and keep our places. Cyra said she would run for food a few minutes before the clinic was scheduled to start up again.

"Good plan. So how was your date?"

Cyra grinned at me. "He seems nice. Took me to dinner and a movie. We had a drink afterward. He wanted a kiss.Just a little smack on the lips, and that was it."

"Will you see him again?"

Cyra laughed, "I have to! He works at the club."

I raised my eyebrows.

"He's the dishwasher, slash maintenance man, slash go-fer."

"Isn't it a little uncomfortable for you to date a guy you work with? I mean, your job is to take off your clothes and get men excited... I mean, well..." I was fumbling for the right words.

"I get it," Cyra cut me off. "But it's a show. There are rules to it. Sure, the men can put money in our clothes, or what's left of them, but they can't touch us other than that. We aren't allowed to have a drink with them or to socialize with them. They can't wait for us after work. We have bouncers who keep everything under control. Our management is tight."

"I'm sorry," I said. "I just wondered. Don't you think he might be jealous, or something?"

"Hey, it's just one date! Although he did ask me out again. We aren't even supposed to date employees. If the owner found out, we might lose our job. So he's gotta be cool."

"But you like him?"

"Yeah, from what I know. Hey, look. Lunch break is almost over. I'll go get us something. The menu said chili. Are you game?"

"Anything called food will do. I brought a thermos if you want black coffee."

"Deal."

Cyra returned in a few minutes with four slices of pizza. "There are so many people here, they ran out of chili and had to send out for pizzas!" Cyra said.

"I like pizza!" I said and laughed.

The outing was a success. Danielle and Ben and Martin immediately began to plan, each in their own way, a musical freestyle ride for the first show of the season. Danielle was quiet, but Ben and Martin talked so much about the clinic on the way home that I threatened to stop posting events. I was joking, of course.

However, the next event wasn't as popular. It was a

saddle fitting clinic held at a farm in Oxford. Only Cyra and I and two working students, Meghan and Mitch, attended. I thought that Meghan and Mitch signed up to be able to spend the day together. Bonnie paid their admission, but she didn't attend, so I drove everyone to the clinic.

The last outing we scheduled before the show season started was a conformation clinic presented by the staff of a veterinary clinic in Metamora. The twins, several boarders, and all the working students went. We enjoyed a live presentation of good and poor conformation and learned how to compensate for those weaknesses and prevent injuries in training.

For two days following the clinic, Ben and Martin went through the barn, comparing the handouts they received at the clinic with horses boarded at Centerline.

Finally, I asked them, "Are you two thinking about becoming veterinarians?"

Martin and Ben looked at each other.

"We were thinking about it," Ben said.

"Now we don't think we will," Martin said.

"This is serious stuff," Ben said.

"We want to find something fun to do!" Martin said, and with that said, the twins folded their handouts, stuck them in their back pockets, and walked away.

25 - DINNER TOGETHER

Cyra and I were in the forth week of our pottery class. In the first class, the instructor had shown us examples of what we would make: a bowl, a flower pot, two large flower vases and, for the final project, a 4-piece set of serving dishes. She had given us a list of supplies needed to make the items and suggested that the class partner up and share the cost of tools and materials. Cyra and I looked at each other and smiled.

Then she introduced us to various clays, glazes and dry materials such as sand, dolomite and potash. We learned about the uses of frit, grog, various oxides and carbonates. We were shown tools for cutting, sculpting, modeling, slicing and shaping the clay.

In three sessions, we learned how to use all those materials plus throwing sticks, rollers, rubbers, sponges, brushes, banding wheels, sculpture stands, wax, calipers and tongs. We had learned about all those materials and tools, but we were not proficient in anything.

As we were leaving the third class, Cyra said to me, "Whew! I thought this class would be a breeze! I thought we would just grab a wad of clay, smack it on the wheel, turn it and fire it in an oven! It's a lot harder than that and so much to learn."

"And so much can go wrong after you do all the work." My first flower pot had shattered in the oven.

Cyra shook her head. "Maybe we should have signed up for that class drawing naked people!"

I laughed. "Do you have a date tonight?"

"No," Cyra said, "tonight is all mine."

"Then come to my house and let me make dinner for you," I suggested.

"That's very nice of you," Cyra replied, "but I don't feel Grosse Pointey tonight. Come to my place and we can have hot dogs?"

I frowned. "Okay, my turn to be picky. I don't like hot dogs. Let's get take-out and go to your place."

"Okay." Cyra said.

I suggested we get a takeout order from a German restaurant in Richmond. Cyra agreed, and we called in the order. After getting a little help from the person taking the order, we wound up ordering a feast: spargel (white asparagas) with Hollandaise sauce, bratkartoffeln (pan-roasted potatoes) and sauerbraten (sour roast).

After the cook added bread, plastic dinnerware and napkins, we left the restaurant carrying five bags to the car.

"We have enough food to feed us for a week!" Cyra laughed.

"And to make me diet for a month," I added.

Cyra's home was a rented room on the third floor of an old house. It was a large room, converted from an attic, with a balcony overlooking Main Street and a window that opened to the rooftop of the second floor.

"I like to sit on the balcony with coffee in the morning and get some sun on the rooftop if I'm home in the afternoon," she told me.

Cyra said she shared the bathroom and kitchen, on the second floor with another tenant. "She's a college girl who works part time. She's quiet and very clean, so it works out okay."

We ate on Cyra's balcony and watched traffic go by. "Do you ever wonder about all these people?" Cyra asked me. "Like what kind of lives they lead? Are they rushing home from an office job to make dinner and help the kids with their homework? Do they hate their jobs? Do they get along with their partners? Are the children in trouble all the time, or do they participate in so many sports and hobbies that the parents feel like a taxi service? How about the cost of their clothes? Kids grow up so fast! They cost so much!"

I looked at Cyra. "That sounds pretty depressing. Is that the way you grew up?"

Cyra snorted. "Hardly! I can't remember being a kid. I went to work every day with Gaho, my mother, even before I could walk. We cleaned cabins and motels and did laundry. They said we were home-schooled, but we took our lessons to work and did them there. With nothing else to do but work and study, that's what we did."

I frowned. "You're from Nevada, right? You didn't

attend school?"

"I am a Paiute Indian. We lived near Pyramid Lake in Nevada. Half of us were unemployed, so whenever we could find work, we took it."

"Oh. I didn't know. How many were in your family?"

"It was just our mother, Gaho, my sister, Ituha, and me. My sister left when I was four. She was twelve. After she left, it was just Gaho and me. We lived in a shack in the desert. We always carried water home with us from work because our house had no plumbing and water was hard to find in the desert, anyway. We rode our horses to work." Cyra smiled.

"And where was your dad?" I asked.

Cyra snorted again. "Never met him. My mother wouldn't talk about him. She hated men. I think my sister had a different father. She is tall and I am short. She has red skin, like my mother. Mine is more brown."

I looked at Cyra. "I guess I can see a brownish tone to your skin. I can't really tell."

"Make-up." Cyra said with a crooked smile and pointed to her cheek.

"Did your sister come home to visit? Did you see her much?" I asked.

Cyra turned to look at me. "I saw her when I was ten years old, when she came and took me away. That was it. She was eighteen, and all grown up. She was beautiful."

"She took you away? Where? To live with her?"

Cyra turned her face to the window. "She took me to Reno. To work. She just left me there. I didn't know where she was for six years. It took me a while, but I found her." Cyra nodded with a frown.

"What happened to your mother? Do you visit her often?" I thought of my mother, living in Richmond in a garage apartment. Wednesday was my mother's only day off, but I had missed the last Wednesday. I felt guilty about that.

"I saw my mother only twice after I went away. I had to catch a ride. I wasn't allowed to leave work, so I had to sneak out. The last time I saw her, she was very sick. She died a month later. She told me she had pneumonia when I saw her, but it was cancer." Cyra shook her head.

"I'm sorry." I said and, without thinking about it, I touched Cyra on her shoulder.

Cyra moved away from my hand and put her back to me. She stared at the traffic on the street below. "I didn't know where my sister was then. I couldn't tell her our mother had died."

"That's awful," I said.

Cyra took a deep breath and continued, "After our mother died, I was determined to find my sister. And I did. When I found her, and knew approximately where she was, I made plans. It took me years to catch up with her, but I did."

Cyra turned around and looked at me. "I don't know why I'm telling you all this. I never tell anyone about it."

"That's okay. I'm a good listener and I have a short memory." I smiled at Cyra.

Cyra stood up. "Okay. Enough. I'm gonna make us some coffee. There's a good movie at the Chesterfield Cinema. Wanna go?"

"Sure!" I didn't ask what was playing.

After the movie, which had been a comedy about aliens, we had coffee and cheesecake at a restaurant in New Haven. On the way back to Cyra's place, I drove by my mother's apartment and pointed it out to Cyra.

"My mother lives there," I said, slowing the car.

Cyra craned her neck for a look. "Nice house!"

I giggled. "Not the house! The garage!"

"Your mother lives in a garage?"

There was no traffic behind us, so I pulled over to the curb. "No, sorry, not the garage. In an apartment above the garage. You can see her porch from here."

"Oh! Cool. I see it now. She lives alone?"

"Yep. She never married. I'd drive in and introduce you, but it's late for her. She gets up at 5 am for work. I'll take you to meet her someday. We can have lunch at the restaurant where she works."

Cyra nodded and smiled. "That would be nice."

26 - THE MYSTERY REVEALED

Two days later, I was walking to the back paddock to get Real when I heard someone scream, "Get away from me!"

I held my breath, but there was nothing more, so I continued walking. Maybe a horse had stepped on someone's foot. That happened once in a while.

But a minute later, I heard Cyra yell, "You're sorry? So what? I'm sorry I ever met you! Get out of my life!"

I dropped my lead rope and ran toward the sound. When I found Cyra in the barn aisle, she was sitting on the floor with her legs drawn up, her face buried in her knees. She was crying.

Irene was standing by her horse, Parcel, who was on crossties.

"What happened?" I asked Irene.

Irene threw her brush down and growled, "I don't have to put up with this! I'm going to talk to Bonnie right now! I'm going to get the trash out of this barn!" she said, pointing at Cyra. Then she headed toward the barn office, leaving her horse standing in the crossties.

Layne cautiously emerged from the tackroom.

I turned and faced Layne. "What happened? Tell me what happened?"

Layne shrugged. "I don't really know. Cyra came

into the barn and this guy followed her. He grabbed her and she pulled away from him. She yelled, 'Let go of me!' and he said, 'You owe me!' Then she yelled, 'Get your hands off me, I don't owe you anything' Then he hit her! I mean, he punched her good! Then he said, 'I'm sorry! I'm so sorry!' and Cyra yelled back, 'You're sorry? Nobody touches me! Nobody hits me!' and she started crying. So then he grabbed her by the shoulders and said, 'I'm sorry, I said I was sorry!' He shook her and Cyra started fighting and screaming for him to get away from her and get out of her life!"

Layne let out a little laugh. "I was in the tackroom and decided to stay there!"

Layne took the saddle off Irene's horse, unsnapped the crossties and put him in his stall. Then she came back to me and said, "I'd better get down to the office and sit on Irene."

I turned to Cyra. I crouched down beside her and said, "Cyra." When she didn't answer, I touched her shoulder. Cyra pushed my hand away and continued to cry. I withdrew my hand but did not get up.

I stayed crouched by Cyra as she continued to cry, her head buried in her knees and her crying coming out in gasping sobs. My legs grew tired, so I sat down by her. Eventually, our shoulders touched. When Cyra did not move away, I leaned a little into her and she pressed back. After a while, she stopped crying and rubbed her face, smearing her eye makeup.

"Here." I reached into my pocket and pulled out

a tissue. Cyra took it and sighed. I wanted to ask a lot of questions but said nothing. After a while Cyra straightened her back and looked up at the ceiling.

"Want to go for a trail ride?" I asked.

Cyra turned and looked at me. After a minute she said, "Sure" in a quiet voice.

"I have to go get Real. Where is Chimmy?"

"In the back pasture."

"Okay. Let's go get them." I got up and extended my hand to Cyra. She looked at it without looking at me, and took it. I pulled her up and we walked out of the barn in silence. I picked up my lead rope along the way.

Back in the barn, Cyra bridled Chimmy. I saddled Real without brushing him and put his snaffle bridle on. We were leading the horses down the aisle when we ran into Irene, who was being followed by Layne and Bonnie.

"I won't put up with trash like you!" Irene shouted at Cyra. "I will not!" Then she stomped out of the barn and headed toward the parking lot. We heard her Maserati start up and gravel flying as she sped out of the parking lot.

Cyra looked at Layne and Bonnie.

Bonnie said, "Go for your ride and we will discuss this tomorrow."

Cyra hung her head.

"Don't think about it another minute," Bonnie said.

"Go enjoy your ride because we can't change what just happened. We will discuss it tomorrow in private."

"Do I have to move my horse?" Cyra asked in a quiet voice.

"Certainly not!" Bonnie said. "But this can't happen again. No more foul language and no more emotional outbreaks unless I cause them!" Bonnie chuckled.

Cyra looked up at Bonnie and smiled sadly.

"I didn't know he was coming here," Cyra said. "I didn't invite him here."

"I understand. I don't want to know your private life," Bonnie told her. "I don't want to know anyone's private life. That's not any of my business."

Cyra blinked her thanks at Bonnie. Behind Bonnie, Layne made the "up" sign with her thumb.

Cyra relaxed a little, and we led our horses out of the barn.

I had Real tacked up in saddle and bridle, but Cyra had only a simple bitless bridle on Chimmy. The bridle was made from a piece of leather that went behind Chimmy's ears, down the sides of her face and circled around her nose and chin, and then became one rein.

I looked at Cyra. "That's an interesting bridle."

"I made it when I took lessons at the barn in Reno. Sometimes I need the freedom to ride without a bit or saddle. Chimmy's fine with it. I guide her with my knees and thighs."

"Okay," I shrugged. "But you forgot to bring your

helmet."

"I never wear a helmet unless I'm in a lesson or at a show." Cyra said. "I hate them!"

I could see that Cyra was coming back to herself and continued the conversation. "Bonnie doesn't insist that you always wear one?"

"No. Michigan law says that an adult can choose to wear one or not. I choose not. I wear one for Bonnie out of respect when I train with her, but I've ridden my whole life without a helmet. I can't stand them!"

I smiled. "Okay if I wear one?"

Cyra smiled back, "Sure!"

We walked the horses to the outdoor arena and Cyra grabbed Chimmy's mane in her left hand and swung up on her back with one easy bounce off the ground.

I led Real to the mounting block and fumbled with the stirrup. Feeling awkward after watching Cyra's graceful spring up and onto her horse's back, I climbed aboard Real.

We followed the trail behind the outdoor arena. It was a warm afternoon and the sun cast a transparent golden glow all around us. along the way, I spotted wild ginger budding up to flower. Bloodwort and trillium also promised to reveal flowers soon.

Cyra noticed that I was looking at the new growth and pointed to a plant on her right. "That's wild garlic. Some people call it garlic mustard. It's supposed to be good for your heart if you eat it, but Layne and I keep pulling it out because it will take over everything if you don't control it. And you have to put it in the garbage when you pull it out. It will re-seed just lying on the ground if you don't!"

"Sounds obnoxious," I said.

"Yeah, like some people." Cyra grumbled.

"So what was that all about, anyway?" I thought the comment about "some people" was a good opening.

"Oh, Irene wants me gone!" Cyra told me.

"No, I mean about that guy. Who is he? Who is he to you?"

Cyra stopped her horse and turned around to frown at me. I thought I had crossed an invisible line, but Cyra said, "He's my, no, he was my boyfriend. The guy I've been dating."

"Was is obvious!" I smiled. "Did he hurt you? Physically?"

"Well, he hit me. He wanted me to go to his place last night after work. You know. But I wouldn't. So he had a fit, but I just drove off. Then he came here today. Said I 'owed him'! You were right. He got jealous and possessive. But no one owns me and no one hits me!" Cyra said fiercely. Tears were popping out of her eyes even though she wasn't crying.

"I'm sorry he treated you that way," I said. "Please don't let men break your spirit. Maybe you can get some other line of work?"

"I can't. It's all I know, and it's the only way I can make the money I need. I couldn't support Chimmy, go to school and save up for Florida unless I make good money. And anyway, most men are assholes, no matter what kind of work you do."

I didn't know what to say. I didn't know anything about men. I decided to focus on Florida. "I'm glad you're going to Florida. But I'll miss you. Does anyone know you're going besides me?"

"No. I talked to Bonnie about it and she wants me to go, but some of the others might not like it when they see the list posted next week. Don't say anything. Anyway, I need to save up a lot of money between now and then to go. It might not happen. So don't say anything."

"I won't."

Cyra let out a big sigh and said, "Come on, let's ride," and took off at a canter. I followed with a smile.

Soon, we came to the stream and slowed to a walk. Cyra stopped Chimmy a few feet into the stream and jumped down into the water. She bent over and picked up something and handed it to me.

It was a bright pink and yellow rock about the size of a chicken's egg. "It's beautiful," I said.

"I always take a rock when I cross the stream."

Cyra picked up another rock, grabbed a handful of Chimmy's mane and swung up onto her back and we continued the ride.

We cantered across the meadow, as I had done with Layne, and trotted into the woods on the other side, then walked. The trail had been groomed recently and the horse's feet made soft, comforting sounds as they walked on it.

"Who keeps the trail groomed?" I asked.

"This is state land," Cyra told me. "State workers keep it groomed for hikers and horses."

"Oh, and I imagine people walk their dogs out here too?"

"Not often. You see them once in a while, but they have to keep the dogs on a leash. Most people don't like that and take their dogs someplace like a dog park where they can let them run free." Cyra bent down and buried her nose in Chimmy's neck. "I love the smell of horses."

"Me too," I replied. "But I have to take my clothes off in the mudroom and shower right away when I come home. My husband doesn't want the house smelling like a horse."

"Did you ever smell the colors of horses?"

I raised my eyebrows at Cyra.

"Seriously!" Cyra said, and laughed. "A grey horse smells a certain way and a brown horse smells another way. A red horse smells different than a black horse. A pinto smells differently in the different colors of his coat. Do you think I'm nuts?"

"Well, no. But I never thought about it," I bent over to smell Real. Then I walked him closer to Chimmy and put my nose on Chimmy's neck, then back on Real.

"Wow, you're right! They smell totally different! So two horses might smell different, just like two people might smell different? And with horses, it's their color that makes them smell different?"

"I think so. Maybe that's why insects seem to bug dark horses more than light-colored ones. They have a stronger smell. Anyway, we can test it out when we get back to the barn. We can run around and smell all the horses!" Cyra laughed and took off at a trot. I followed, laughing.

Soon we came to the little clearing with the statue of the Indian girl and the deer. Cyra stopped and slid off Chimmy. She just dropped her rein and Chimmy stood, ground-tied, and watched her.

Cyra walked up to the circle of rocks and placed her rock in the circle. Then she walked to the statue and put her hand on the deer's head.

I tied Real's reins to a tree branch and followed her. I bent down to put my rock in the circle of rocks.

"This place means a lot to me," Cyra said as she turned to watch me put the pink rock in the circle.

I walked over to the statue and stood by Cyra. "What do you mean it 'means a lot'?"

"Because I'm Indian." Cyra looked at me. "Maybe no one knows or cares. Maybe they just don't notice because they never get beyond the make-up."

"Maybe. Or maybe it doesn't matter."

"It matters to me. I was born on a reservation near Pyramid Lake. I told you about our home, but I didn't tell you it's a reservation. I told you that I left when I was ten. Anyway, Layne and I made this little clearing and put the statue and rocks here. It reminds me of my mother. And it reminds me of why I'm here."

I stopped breathing, but hoped that Cyra didn't notice. Layne had told me no one knew who put the statue here. Why? And what did Cyra mean by "why I'm here"? I took a deep breath and said, "Are you telling me you're Indian because you tell everyone? Or is that a secret, too?"

"You and Layne know. I don't want anyone else to know. Not yet."

I dropped my eyes. "Oh. Thank you for telling me, but I wouldn't worry about it if I were you," I said.

"I'm not worried and you're not me."

I looked at Cyra to see if she was hurt or angry, but she didn't appear to be either.

We rode back to the barn in silence, just looking at the landscape, listening to the birds and the sounds our horse's feet made on the trail.

After putting our horses in their stalls, I said, "Let's go smell some horses?"

Cyra laughed, "Sure!"

So we went from stall to stall, putting our noses up against the horse's necks and, in the case of Puzzles, all over his tri-colored body. The horses seemed amused by our strange behavior.

"What do you think?" Cyra asked me.

"I think my nose is dirty!" I laughed. "But yes, the dark brown horses smell rich like chocolate, the greys smell minty, and the chestnuts smell spicy!"

"Exactly!" Cyra laughed. "Now you're crazy too!"

I looked at Cyra, thinking how good it was to see her laughing again after the terrible morning. "How about dinner and a movie again? "

"Sure," Cyra said. "You're a great date!"

When I finally got home, it was 11 pm. Al had been in New York, and I was surprised when I saw his car in the garage. I walked straight through the kitchen and into the entertainment room without taking off my riding clothes and boots. Al was sitting in his recliner, having a drink.

"Al!" was all I could say as I bent down and hugged him. He did not return the hug.

"Where have you been?" he asked without warmth.

I was surprised at his tone and surprise quickly turned into anger when I thought how he hadn't called since he left, not even to tell me he was coming home. "I went to the barn, to dinner, to the movies, had coffee and came home. Do I need to supply witnesses?"

Al seemed to relax a little. "No. I've been sitting here since seven, waiting for you. I was getting annoyed, then I got worried, then I got angry," Al explained.

"Why didn't you call?"

"I did."

I pulled my cell phone from the pouch on my belt. "Oh. It died. I didn't know. Look," and I showed Al the black screen. I tried to boot it up. It started up, then failed. "Sorry." Tears were forming in my eyes. I had never before lost my temper with Al.

Al reached up and grabbed me, pulling me down on top of him. "I missed you, and I got a little drunk, waiting." He put his face in my hair.

I put my arms around him. "I missed you too."

Al stroked my hair and rubbed my back. Then he kissed me and hugged me again.

After snuggling in his arms for a while, I asked, "Are you finished with the case or do you have to go back?"

"Finished. We got an acquittal. I'm home now. Home to get acquainted with my wife again." Al sniffed. "Or to get acquainted with who she has become."

"Oh! I forgot to take off my riding clothes when I saw your car in the garage." I pinched his nose. "Hold on, I'll be right back."

Relaxing in his arms that night, I thought, This is the man I fell in love with. It's good to have him home again. I forgot about thoughts of Al with other women. When he was with me, I felt he was mine one hundred percent.

27 - GOING TO FLORIDA

It was the last week in May and Cyra and I were working on the final project for our pottery class. We were required to create a four-piece set of serving dishes consisting of a twelve inch round platter, a low serving bowl, a deep serving bowl and a platter with a divided well.

I decided to make my dishes in white bone china with no design beyond a simple oval shape. I felt the design would be perfect in my lifeless dining room.

Cyra was artistic, but stayed within the guidelines required by the final project. Her dishes would be dark grey with blue flecks. "For Chimmy's color," she told me. Her design was "organic" or irregular in shape. She had brushed a texture comb in long, flowing strokes from the center of the dishes to the edges. "To remind me of Chimmy's long mane and tail," she said.

"Very nice," I told her. "I'm just not a creative thinker."

"Well, this class is just to finish the requirements for my associate's degree, so I think it's okay to play a little."

"What will you do when you get it?"

"Nothing. It's not good for anything. It's just a piece of paper. It won't get me a good job. I have to decide if

I want to go on for a bachelor's or quit."

"I got my associate's degree and a certificate as a paralegal. You could do the same thing."

"After I finish this class and get my associate's, I'm gonna take a break. I'm going to the sanctioned shows this summer and to train and show in Florida this winter."

"So, you're still going? Did you talk to Bonnie?"

"Yep. I talked to Bonnie. She wants me to go, and I have enough money saved for the deposit." Cyra frowned. "Irene will have a fit."

"So, let her! That's her problem, isn't it?" I sighed. Why did Irene have to be such a bitch?

Cyra was right. Two days later, Bonnie posted the list of boarders going to Florida for the winter. The list was always posted before June 1st, reminding those who were going that housing and stabling fees had to be paid by July 1st and full payment for training and coaching fees were due on September 1st.

Irene had what my mother would call a "melt down". The twins and I were reading the notice soon after Bonnie pinned it to the corkboard by the office door when Irene walked up, quickly scanned the list, and choked.

"Cyra?" she hissed. "I don't believe it!" She jerked open the door to the office, marched in and slammed it shut. Her voice was clearly audible on the other side of the door and Ben, Martin, and I listened without shame.

"That's a joke, right?" Irene was livid. "WHO put Cyra's name on the list for Florida?'

"No, it's not a joke. Cyra's going to Florida," Susan told Irene. "She's very excited about it. "

"I CANNOT believe this!" Irene must have slammed something down on the desk because we heard a thud and then Bonnie shouting, "Irene, that's enough! I will NOT have you act like this toward my mother!"

"Cyra is TRASH!" Irene growled, probably at Bonnie.

"She ISN'T!" Susan joined the argument. "She wears too much makeup for you? Or is it her job you don't approve of? She's a talented rider, she has a good horse, AND she's a good person. She's going, so get over it!"

"I can't BELIEVE that you expect me to share my time in Florida with TRASH!" Irene abruptly opened the office door and rushed out, almost colliding with me and the twins. She slammed the door and marched down the aisle toward the parking lot. The twins broke into giggles and smothered them in their hands.

Bonnie opened the office door after a few moments. She peeked out and looked down the aisle to see Irene leaving the barn. Then she looked at me and the twins. "That was fun, wasn't it?" she said and smiled.

Ben, Martin and I laughed with relief.

At the same time, Layne came down the aisle with a

lead rope. "What's so funny?" she asked.

"Oh," Bonnie said laughing, "Dressage Queen just found out that her worst nightmare is going to Florida with us," and she pointed to the list on the corkboard.

Layne looked at the list and, instead of smiling she frowned. "Oh!" she said. "Where's Irene?"

Bonnie pointed, "Parking lot. I think she's leaving."

Layne dropped the lead rope, spun around, ran down the aisle and out the door to the parking lot.

Bonnie was puzzled. "Hummm, I thought Layne would get a big kick out of that! Guess I was wrong."

The twins looked at each other and shrugged. I dropped my eyes and studied my shoes.

Susan appeared at the office door. "Okay, Fun's over. Let's get back to the paperwork, Bonnie."

Later in the afternoon, I saw Layne tacking up Irene's Grand Prix horse. "Are you riding Parcel?" I didn't know Layne rode Parcel. I thought only Bonnie and Irene rode him.

"Yes. I'll be riding him now whenever she can't or doesn't feel like it. And her young horse, too."

"Wow. That's great."

Layne leaned toward me. "Want to know a secret?"

"Sure!" I brightened. Sometimes Layne could be a lot of fun.

"I'm dying to tell someone other than my husband and you're the only one I can trust!"

This was sounding like something serious, not fun.

244

"What?" I said, frowning.

"This is a secret, so you can't tell anyone, okay?"

"Sure. I have a short memory," I tried to joke, but it sounded lame.

"Irene just texted me that she's in a real estate agent's office, looking at farms for sale! I got her to look at some farms last week and this thing about Florida made her so mad that she's at the agent's office, looking at more farms right now, as we speak!"

"What?" I was confused.

"You remember, on our shopping trip, Irene hinted at making an investment? We've been talking about starting our own barn. Boarding, training, imports and sales, you know. We looked at a few places last week, and now she's got the bug. She's convinced that we can build an elite business! We're gonna buy a farm!"

"You're going out on your own in a business with Irene? I thought you said you might do that after you reach Grand Prix and get your gold medal. Or maybe after training in Europe."

"Well, I'd rather have my own place, and the sooner the better, as far as I'm concerned. This morning did it for Irene. She said she's tired of rubbing shoulders with scum and being told what to do."

"Wow," was all I could say.

"So, get ready! Maybe you can move with us!"

"Oh, I don't know. Where would you be located?" I didn't intend to move, but I wanted to be polite.

"We're looking in the Oxford and Metamora area.

That's where all the money is! Come with us and you can spend time with quality people!"

"Oh. That's probably too far away. I live in Grosse Pointe. It would take me too long to get there." I was really thinking I was glad that their farm wouldn't be close.

"Exactly! You're Grosse Pointe! You're white collar. Aren't you tired of spending time with blue collars?" Layne winked at me.

I smiled tightly and took a deep breath. I looked Layne in the eye. "Maybe you haven't noticed, Layne. My collar is blue." Then I turned away and walked into the tackroom.

In the tackroom I stood for a minute. I was confused and angry. I felt that Layne had betrayed Bonnie.

I thought Layne should have told Bonnie that she and Irene were looking at farms. I didn't expect loyalty from a person like Irene, but Layne surprised me. And I surprised myself with my reply to Layne about blue collars. I was glad I said it. I stood for a while with my hand on my saddle, just breathing and feeling my heart rate return to normal.

When would Layne tell Bonnie? Now that I knew their secret, I felt like a traitor. I debated about going to Susan and Bonnie with the news, but finally decided that, if Layne's loyalty could be bought with money, Susan and Bonnie were better off without her. They would know what to do when the time came.

... *continued in* **THE HORSE CONNECTION** part 2

also by Charlotte Godfrey:

Loving Mother
and leaving her at any cost based on a true story

Life with Dutch
living with a grouchy Amazon parrot

BOARDING STABLE RANTS
why barn owners are crazy!

Learn to Ride!
Introducing horse care and riding

ROADAPPLES...
Droppings from a lifetime with horses...

FABULOUS FORWARDS
14 years of e-mail fun

AGING FORWARDS
From Fabulous Forwards

THE HORSE CONNECTION part 2
horses, friendship and revenge

THE HORSE CONNECTION part 3
growing pains

Loving Mother
and leaving her at any cost

"Your mother has had an accident and you need to come home."

Home. There was that word again. My shoulders dropped. Would I ever be free of this woman? Every time I thought I had gotten free, I found myself returning home again. I let out a deep sigh. I had been stupid to think that I could be free.

"Is she gonna die?" I asked.

"No, but she needs 24 hour care."

It suddenly occurred to me that I would have to be the caregiver. My breathing stopped. I felt my stomach knot up. Was there any escape from this woman? Would my life always be tied to hers? 24 hour care? I couldn't breathe.

LIFE WITH DUTCH

life with a 20 year old grouchy Amazon parrot

I'm a 76 year old woman who adopted a 20 year old Amazon parrot. I am approaching the end of my life but a 20 year old Amazon parrot is just beginning middle age. I guess I thought I'd have to decide who gets to care for the bird when I'm gone. But, as it turned out, the bird decided that one.

I am retired and living alone in an apartment and I got the bright idea of adopting a parrot. I guess you could say I was lonely and looking for trouble. I found it.

Dutch had been in the same home with his owner, a man, for 20 years. The first owner died and the surviving relatives sent Dutch to a rescue. That should have told me something.

The name "Dutch" should have also told me something. It's an old fashioned slang word meaning "trouble."

I went to the rescue looking for an African Grey parrot. I owned a Grey and a Amazon when I was younger. Much younger. The Grey was intelligent, talkative and had a gentle nature. The Amazon was aggressive and loud. Maybe I didn't remember that.

Anyway, the rescue didn't have a Grey, but it had an Amazon for adoption: Dutch. I visited with Dutch for a month before adopting him, and he bit me, but only once. It didn't draw blood, and I shrugged it off. The old saying is "If you own a parrot, it's not a question of if you're gonna be bitten, but when."

The surviving relatives, who dropped Dutch off at the rescue, didn't leave a written history. The rescue told me he had been the property of a man for 20 years, preferred men, and was adopted by another man and returned to the rescue after 5 days. That should have told me something. But...

The rescue said the man who adopted him had 3 dogs and Dutch had become aggravated because of them and was returned. That made sense to me at the time, but I realized later that Dutch could make short work of three dogs.

In addition, there was no vet history for Dutch, no evidence that he knew how to speak and his wings were fully clipped.

I don't have any dogs or cats. I live in a small apartment by myself so, I adopted Dutch.It wasn't long before I thought I would have been happier with a pit bull or a tarantula.

BOARDING STABLE RANTS

why barn owners are crazy!

FORWARD

This book was written after 45 years in the business of boarding horses. It was born out of hard work, joys and tears, fights and victories, rescues, puzzelments and bitch sessions.

I hope it will make you smile or laugh. If it makes you angry, maybe I've hit a nerve or fleshed out a truth.

The truth is that it's difficult to be a boarder who has to trust someone else to care for their most precious animal and it's difficult to be a boarding stable owner who has to balance all the aspects of running a business with being an unpaid psychologist.

And now that I've managed to ruffle the feathers of both boarders and boarding stable owners, let's see if I can do some more damage in the following pages...

DEDICATION

This book is dedicated to the memory of my husband, Joel, who firmly believed that horses were livestock until the day we divorced.

NOTE

In this book, I refer to the boarding stable owner and the boarder as "you". I might not be referring directly to you as the subject of my rant but, I could be if the shoe fits!

I'm gonna step on a few toes. I've been in this business too long to be nice about the issues in this book. I've wrangled with them almost every day of my life for the last 45 years and it's time to vent, so put on your shit-kickin' boots and join me!

Learn to Ride!
Introducing horse care and riding

TO THE NEW HORSEMAN:

Learn to Ride! is a guide, written for young horsemen, but it has been proven to be useful and fun for new horsemen of any age. I suggest that any new horseman of any age find an instructor to act as a mentor when using this guide.

Please write in this book:
There is a place for your name and places to make notes. There are questions throughout the book about each chapter. You can answer the questions - either with your instructor or at home by yourself. Some questions are about things not discussed in this book. I asked them to make you THINK and to discuss them with your instructor or find the answers online. It's fun to not know something and learn the answer!

With the help of this book, searching online or asking your instructor, you will learn to halter, groom, show a horse in-hand, help tack up your horse and ride a beginner dressage test.

Welcome to the wonderful world of horses!

Charlotte Godfrey

ROADAPPLES...
TABLE OF CONTENTS

FABULOUS FORWARDS
14 years of forwarding fun!

INTRODUCTION

It was the year 2000 and I didn't know how to turn on a computer. That was fine with my husband. He wanted me at home, taking care of him and pretty much ignorant of the outside world, except for TV news, which was unavoidable since he watched it every night. But I was curious and I requested a computer for Christmas. My husband brought home an old desktop from his workplace with Windows 94 on it. No internet.

I asked my girlfriend, Sandi, to give me a lesson on computers, "Teach me how a computer works," I said. She giggled and rubbed her hands together. "Okay! Welcome to the modern world! This is how you turn it on. Now what do you want to do?"

"I don't know." I said, "Just teach me a little about them." So, she proceeded to tell me that computers are based on files and folders, and my eyes glazed over. First typing, then files and folders? Ugh. I hated typing in high school and barely passed the class. Files and folders? It sounded boring.

But she continued to teach me. Computers, she said, can be highly organized tools. I really like organization. So I learned about files and folders and I became a fairly good typist.

By January, I was longing to be on the internet and find out what the big deal was, so I called a dial-up company and got online. Then the emails started coming in from all my computer savy friends! What a hoot! The fun was unbelievable! So I copied the best forwards, pasted them into files and put them in folders... for fourteen years!

 Now it appears that texting is replacing emailing friends and the once enjoyable experience of email has become a slush pile of advertisement and con artist scams. I came to realize that I had enjoyed an "era" which has pretty much passed.

This book is an effort to preserve, in my own way, the fun that emailing once gave us. I urge you to copy some of these forwards and send them to your friends. Have fun!

AGING FORWARDS
14 years of forwarding fun!

LIFE BEGINS AT FIFTY

Maybe it's true that life begins at fifty...
But thats when everything else starts to wear out,
fall out, or spread out.

about the author:

Charlotte Godfrey's first horse was her Grandpop's mule, Maggie, who she jumped bareback - until Pop found her on the ground after jumping an obstacle under Granny's wire clothes line. When he discovered that she wasn't decapitated, he forbade her to jump and bought her a horse who tried to kill her in other ways. That horse, who knew several ways of getting rid of children, taught her about self-preservation and confirmed in her a life-long love of horses and dressage.

*photograph by
Michael Sexton*

Her next horse, after a child, college, marriage, divorce and re-marriage (in that order, but repeat a few steps...) was a Quarter Horse named Oliver, who was obtained by blackmailing her husband and threatening the owner. After Charlotte added 2 more horses to the board bill, her husband decided that it would be cheaper and more tax-advantageous to buy property and build their own boarding stable! He built a barn, purchased a horse trailer, dug a pond, constructed an outdoor arena, an indoor arena, more stalls...and so on...

Running a boarding stable proved to be such a delightful way to lose money that, after her divorce, Charlotte and 2 unfortunate partners: Mike and her mother, Milly, joined up to buy an even bigger boarding stable.

Charlotte is pictured above with her horse, Gotsno, or "Mr. Wonderful," as he prefers to be known...

If you enjoyed this book, please leave a review. Thanks!

www.ingramcontent.com/pod-product-compliance
Lightning Source LLC
Chambersburg PA
CBHW071456170626
46811CB00007B/2598

* 9 7 9 8 9 9 1 3 9 9 3 3 3 *